WHY DO THE
SEASONS
CHANGE?

WHY DO THE SEASONS CHANGE?

Questions on Nature's Rhythms
and Cycles answered by
the Natural History Museum
Dr Philip Whitfield
& Joyce Pope

Viking Kestrel

VIKING KESTREL
Viking Penguin Inc.,
40 West 23rd Street, New York, New York 10010, U.S.A.
Penguin Books Canada Limited,
2801 John Street, Markham, Ontario, Canada L3R 1B4

Conceived, edited and designed by
Marshall Editions Limited
170 Piccadilly
London W1V 9DD

Editor
Jinny Johnson

Art Editor
Mel Petersen

Picture Editor
Zilda Tandy

Art Assistant
Lynn Hector

Managing Editor
Ruth Binney

Production
Barry Baker
Janice Storr

First published in 1987 by Viking Penguin Inc.
Published simultaneously in Canada

Printed in Portugal
by Printer Portuguesa

2 3 4 5 91 90 89 88

Library of Congress catalog card number: 87-40133
(CIP data available)
ISBN 0-670-81860-7

The Publishers would like to thank the
staff of the Natural History Museum, London,
for their invaluable assistance in the
making of this book.

Contents

Introduction

The world we live in is a truly fascinating place. Just look around you—up at the sky, and down at the ground beneath your feet and you'll begin to wonder why the world is as it is, and how its plants and animals live. Why, for example, does night follow day? Why do the seasons change? And how does a crocus *know* it's spring and time to flower?

The answers to these questions all have one very important thing in common. They rely on the fact that the world around us has many repeating patterns, which are called rhythms and cycles. The time it takes to complete one of these rhythms or cycles can be a few seconds or millions of years—as you'll quickly find out when you begin to read the questions and answers in this book. You'll discover, too, that knowing about these rhythms and cycles really helps make sense of what's going on in the natural world.

Rhythms and cycles are everywhere. Your heart beats regularly inside your chest. You breathe, using an in and out rhythm, every minute of the day, and every day of your life. The Earth you live on has rhythms and cycles, too. The way the Earth goes around the sun brings the cycle of the seasons. The spinning of the Earth itself makes the day and night cycle that all animals and plants live by. The moon's orbit around the Earth drives the ebb and flow of the tides on our planet.

All the plants and animals on Earth, including human beings, reflect these rhythms by being rhythmical themselves. In tune with the rhythms of night and day animals go to sleep or wake up, flowers open or close. As the seasons change, leaves fall, young are born, buds open, birds lay eggs—all at the proper times.

There are rhythms within us, too. "Body clocks" in our heads tick with a daily rhythm and make us wake and feel sleepy at regular times.

Living things and the world that brought them into being pose hundreds of fascinating questions that are really about all these rhythms and cycles. The pages that follow give the answers to some of them.

Abbreviations used in this book:

cm: centimeter   m: meter   km: kilometer   F: Fahrenheit   C: Centigrade

A billion means one thousand million

1

How old is the universe?

The knowable universe began some 15 to 16 thousand million years ago with an immensely violent explosion—"the Big Bang." Everything in the universe is still feeling the effects of this event and the universe is still expanding.

The "Big Bang" was not destructive. It brought clouds of matter together that formed into galaxies—vast clusters of stars moving together through space. Our own solar system—our own sun and fellow planets—formed within one such galaxy.

2

Where did the Earth come from?

The Earth, along with the other planets and the sun, was probably made from parts of a huge cloud of cold gas and dust in space. Some jolt, perhaps a nearby star exploding, gave the cloud a "kick." This made the cloud get smaller: it was "pulled" in by its own gravity.

At the center of the contracting cloud the sun formed. Its center became so hot and compressed that it started to burn and send out light and heat. The remaining debris circling outside the sun cooled and solidified into planets, moons and asteroids (space rocks).

Our solar system, the sun and its nine planets, was probably formed from a huge cloud of gas and dust. Some jolt started the cloud contracting; at its center the collection of gas that was to become the sun began to form.

Gas and dust cloud

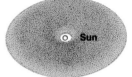

Solid masses begin to form

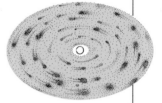

As the cloud got smaller it made a rotating disk of matter. Within that, heavier grains of dust formed cores around which small solid masses began to build up.

3

How old is the Earth?

Our planet is 4,500 million years old. Scientists measure its age by analyzing the oldest rocks in the Earth's crust. Atomic changes take place in rock extremely slowly but we know how long they take. By measuring how much a piece of rock has changed, its age can be worked out.

The oldest rocks from different parts of the world all give much the same result when tested in this way. Tests show that they are all about 4,500 million years old.

Our solar system is in a spiral galaxy like this galaxy (left), with its two satellite galaxies.

How will the universe end?

Just how is not certain but it must end sometime. At the moment the universe is expanding. It may be that this expansion will start to slow down. Then the "pull" of its own gravity will force the universe to start getting smaller again and it will collapse. In the end the whole universe will be compressed into one extraordinarily energetic blob and a new "Big Bang" will occur.

If this idea is right—and it is only one of many—the universe has its own rhythmic beat. Each Big Bang destroys it but also starts off the next cycle of existence.

How long has there been life on Earth?

Earth has been home to some form of life for over 3,000 million years. The earliest forms were similar to today's bacteria. Minute "bugs" like these ruled the world for more than 1,000 million years. Then came more complex creatures and, by 600 to 700 million years ago, there were jellyfish, corals and other creatures in the seas. About 400 million years ago the first fish were swimming in the sea. Some 300 million years ago there were land plants and amphibians, the ancestors of our frogs and toads, crawling among them.

Between 200 and 65 million years ago reptiles ruled the Earth. Among these were the dinosaurs, which included the largest land animals that have ever lived. Manlike apes have only been on Earth relatively recently—for the last 5 million years or so.

Baby planets collide and join

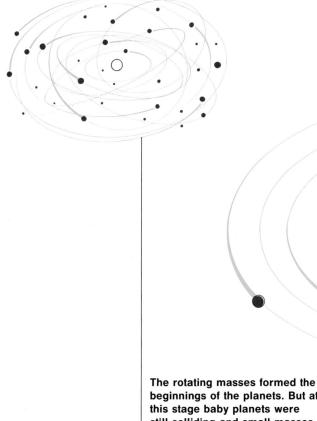

The nine orbiting plants

The rotating masses formed the beginnings of the planets. But at this stage baby planets were still colliding and small masses joining to form larger ones. The sun had begun to give out light and heat.

Nine orbiting planets emerged from the chaos. All the planets, including Earth, orbit the sun in the direction in which the original cloud of dust and gas was spinning.

6

How high is the sky?

When you look up into the daytime sky, what you see, apart from the sun and moon, is the atmosphere of the Earth. The atmosphere is a layer of gases that surrounds Earth and extends some 38 to 50 miles (60 to 80 km) above its surface.

The main gases in the atmosphere are nitrogen, oxygen, carbon dioxide and water vapor. Water vapor forms clouds from which rain and snow come. Most of the clouds you see are in the lower layer of the atmosphere, the troposphere, which extends about 9 miles (15 km) upward.

The sky could be said to be as high as the atmosphere, but that atmosphere gradually merges into interplanetary space. On a clear night you can see stars which are billions of miles away. Suddenly the sky seems to have no boundaries.

7

What are the northern lights?

The northern lights are spectacular patterns of shifting multicolored light. They are seen in the night skies of the northern regions of the world. Similar southern lights are seen near the South Pole.

Also known as the aurora borealis, the northern lights are caused indirectly by the activity of the sun. The outer atmosphere of the sun gives off a solar wind, which carries highly energetic particles. Occasionally solar flares burst out from the sun bringing sudden increases in the wind and giving off more particles.

Carried in the solar wind, the particles are attracted by Earth's magnetism and rain down toward it. Near the magnetic North and South Poles the Earth's magnetism is at its strongest and this funnels the particles from the sun into the top of our atmosphere. Here, the solar wind and the particles meet the gases in the atmosphere and make them glow. This glow is seen as the wonderful display of colored lights known as the aurora.

The strongest displays of northern lights happen after solar flares have sent extra particles into the solar wind.

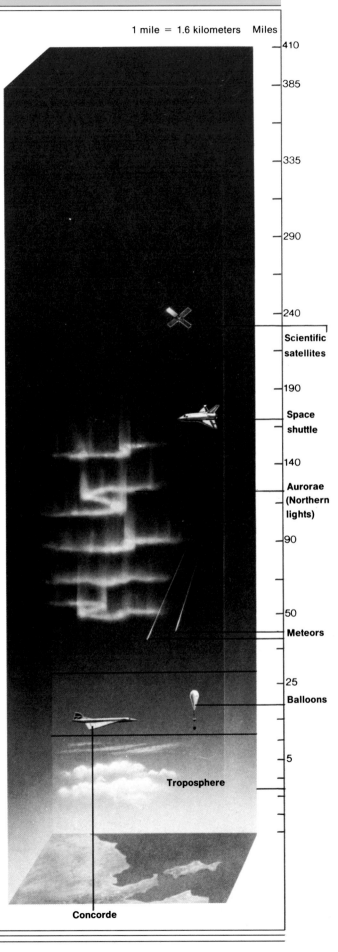

1 mile = 1.6 kilometers   Miles

410
385
335
290
240

Scientific satellites

190

Space shuttle

140

Aurorae (Northern lights)

90

50

Meteors

25

Balloons

5

Troposphere

Concorde

8

What is under the ground?

Just under your feet there is a thin layer of soil. Beneath that is the Earth's crust, with layers of different rocks. The crust is only 5 to 25 miles (8 to 40 km) thick—thinnest under the seabed and thickest at the centers of continents.

Below the crust are 1,800 miles (2,897 km) of liquid rock, then 1,380 miles (2,221 km) of liquid metal. Finally there are 780 miles (1,255 km) of solid metal core.

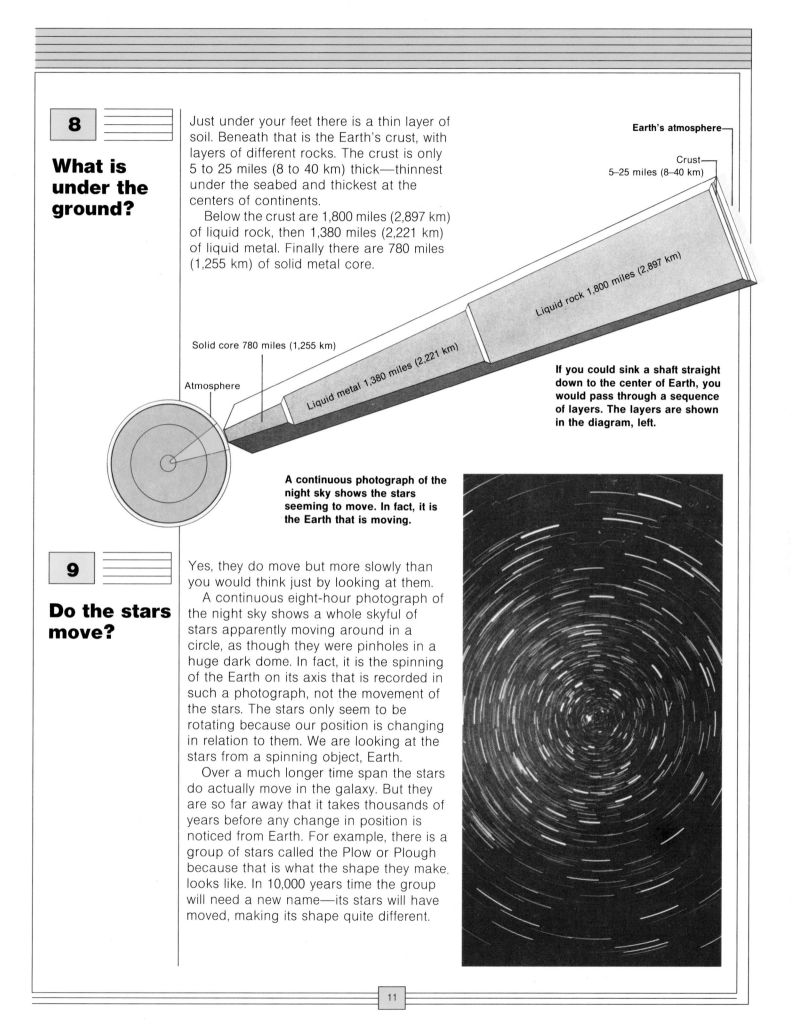

Earth's atmosphere

Crust
5–25 miles (8–40 km)

Liquid rock 1,800 miles (2,897 km)

Liquid metal 1,380 miles (2,221 km)

Solid core 780 miles (1,255 km)

Atmosphere

If you could sink a shaft straight down to the center of Earth, you would pass through a sequence of layers. The layers are shown in the diagram, left.

A continuous photograph of the night sky shows the stars seeming to move. In fact, it is the Earth that is moving.

9

Do the stars move?

Yes, they do move but more slowly than you would think just by looking at them.

A continuous eight-hour photograph of the night sky shows a whole skyful of stars apparently moving around in a circle, as though they were pinholes in a huge dark dome. In fact, it is the spinning of the Earth on its axis that is recorded in such a photograph, not the movement of the stars. The stars only seem to be rotating because our position is changing in relation to them. We are looking at the stars from a spinning object, Earth.

Over a much longer time span the stars do actually move in the galaxy. But they are so far away that it takes thousands of years before any change in position is noticed from Earth. For example, there is a group of stars called the Plow or Plough because that is what the shape they make looks like. In 10,000 years time the group will need a new name—its stars will have moved, making its shape quite different.

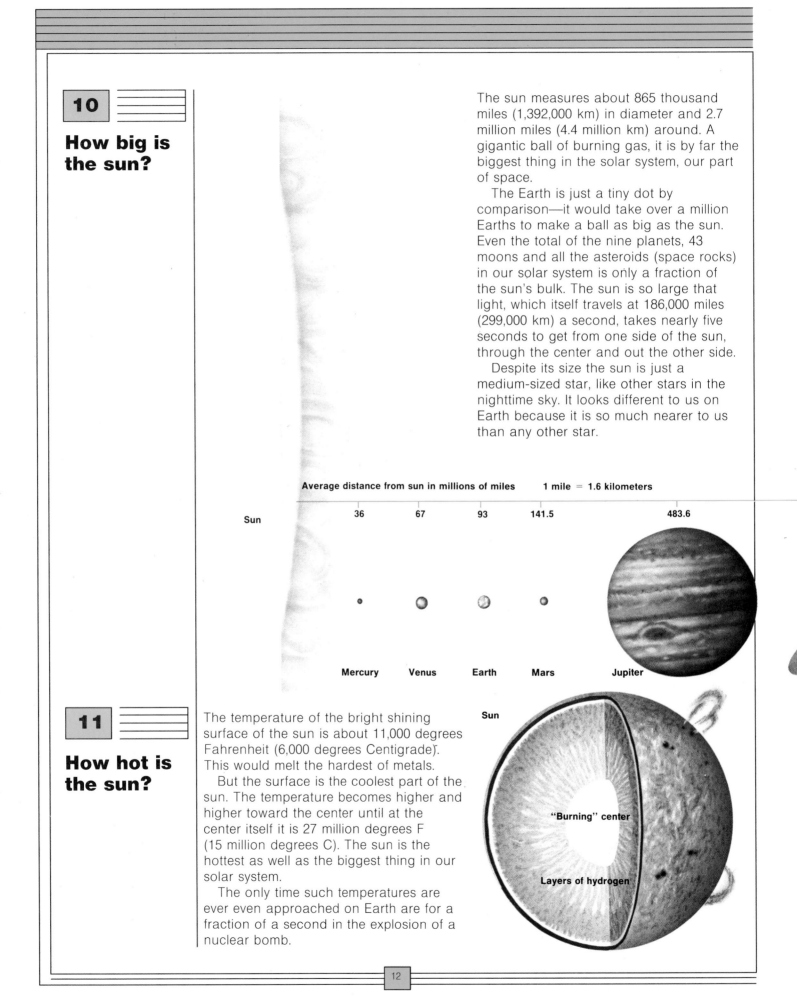

10

How big is the sun?

The sun measures about 865 thousand miles (1,392,000 km) in diameter and 2.7 million miles (4.4 million km) around. A gigantic ball of burning gas, it is by far the biggest thing in the solar system, our part of space.

The Earth is just a tiny dot by comparison—it would take over a million Earths to make a ball as big as the sun. Even the total of the nine planets, 43 moons and all the asteroids (space rocks) in our solar system is only a fraction of the sun's bulk. The sun is so large that light, which itself travels at 186,000 miles (299,000 km) a second, takes nearly five seconds to get from one side of the sun, through the center and out the other side.

Despite its size the sun is just a medium-sized star, like other stars in the nighttime sky. It looks different to us on Earth because it is so much nearer to us than any other star.

Average distance from sun in millions of miles   **1 mile = 1.6 kilometers**

Sun	36	67	93	141.5	483.6
	Mercury	Venus	Earth	Mars	Jupiter

11

How hot is the sun?

The temperature of the bright shining surface of the sun is about 11,000 degrees Fahrenheit (6,000 degrees Centigrade). This would melt the hardest of metals.

But the surface is the coolest part of the sun. The temperature becomes higher and higher toward the center until at the center itself it is 27 million degrees F (15 million degrees C). The sun is the hottest as well as the biggest thing in our solar system.

The only time such temperatures are ever even approached on Earth are for a fraction of a second in the explosion of a nuclear bomb.

Sun

"Burning" center

Layers of hydrogen

What are the planets?

Our planet, Earth, is a rocky ball about 8,000 miles (13,000 km) in diameter and 25,000 miles (40,000 km) around. Earth is just one of the nine planets that go around or orbit our sun.

Planetary orbits are arranged in a particular way. If the sun were the crown of a broad-brimmed hat, the orbits of the planets could be drawn one inside the other on that brim. The planets are all on the same plane or level and they all orbit the sun in the same direction. They also spin as they orbit.

From the sun outward, the planets orbit in the following order: Mercury, Venus, Earth, Mars, Jupiter, Saturn, Uranus, Neptune, Pluto. Between Mars and Jupiter there is a belt of small space rocks or asteroids.

The time that it takes each planet to go around the sun is its year. The farther away a planet is from the sun the longer its orbit and the longer its year. Mercury,

closest to the sun at 36 million miles (58 million km), has a year only 88 days long. The Earth is 93 million miles (150 million km) away from the sun and has a year of 365 and one quarter days. A year on Saturn, 888 million miles (1,429 million km) from the sun, is almost 30 earthly years long, while on Pluto a year is 248 earthly years.

The planets divide into three types according to what they are made of. The four planets nearest the sun are made of rock; Earth is the largest of the group and Mercury the smallest. Beyond the asteroids are the gas giants Jupiter, Saturn, Uranus and Neptune. These are huge cold planets made of liquids and gases, including hydrogen. Jupiter is 1,300 times the size of Earth and the largest of all nine planets.

Tiny distant Pluto, only discovered in 1930, is probably a mixture of ice and rock and the only one of its kind.

| 888 | 1,786.4 | 2,799 | 3,666 |

Saturn   Uranus   Neptune   Pluto

The nine planets in our solar system all go around the sun on their own paths or orbits. Pluto is the most distant at over three and half billion miles (5.9 billion km) from the sun and has an orbit of over 20 billion miles (32 billion km).

In this diagram the planets are shown in proportion to each other and to the massive sun.

What is the sun made of?

The sun is made of "burning" gas. The gas is hydrogen and it burns by the same explosive release of energy that happens in a nuclear bomb.

When hydrogen is squeezed at high enough pressure and temperature the atoms, tiny particles that make up the gas, join together to make another gas, helium. This reaction creates gigantic amounts of energy which is released as light and heat.

At the center of the sun the hydrogen is hot and compressed enough for this nuclear burning to occur. The temperature is 27 million degrees F (15 million degrees C)

and the pressure is immense. It is so great that hydrogen, normally so light it is used to make balloons float in air, is twelve times the weight of lead.

Around the burning center of the sun are more layers of hydrogen. This fuel is enough to keep the sun's fire going for another ten billion years or so. Heat and light from the center are radiated through these layers of gas out into space and keep us warm on Earth.

Beyond the surface of the sun is an atmosphere of thinner gas, the corona, which gives out a dimmer light than the rest of the sun.

Which way does the Earth spin?

Imagine yourself in a spaceship hovering thousands of miles above the North Pole, watching the Earth spinning beneath you. From there you would see that the Earth is moving anticlockwise—the opposite direction to the way a clock's hands move.

One complete spin takes about 24 hours—the earthly day. In each spin, any point on the Earth's surface passes first into the area receiving the sun's rays and then around to the dark, shaded side of the world. So the Earth's spin is the reason for the cycle of day and night.

Except for Venus, all the planets spin in the same direction, but at different speeds. The largest, Jupiter, completes its spin in just under ten hours. Venus is the slowest planet, revolving once every 243 days.

Direction of Earth's spin

The Earth spins anticlockwise and takes 24 hours to complete a spin.

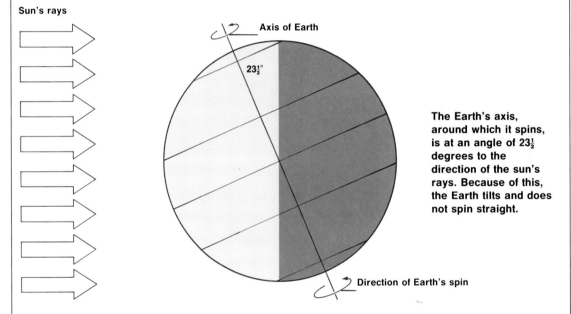

Sun's rays

Axis of Earth

$23\frac{1}{2}°$

The Earth's axis, around which it spins, is at an angle of $23\frac{1}{2}$ degrees to the direction of the sun's rays. Because of this, the Earth tilts and does not spin straight.

Direction of Earth's spin

Does the Earth spin straight?

The Earth spins evenly and steadily around its axis, the imaginary line through its center from the North to the South Pole. In the north, this axis points to the region of the star we call the Pole Star or Polaris.

But this axis is tilted and does not lie at right angles to the direction of the sun's rays, nor to the flat plane of the Earth's orbit. It leans at an angle of $23\frac{1}{2}$ degrees, so the Earth does not spin straight. For half of the year, the northern end of the Earth's axis points slightly toward the sun; for the rest of the year, it points away from it. It is this tilt that produces the seasons on our planet. A tilt away from the sun

brings winter, a tilt toward its rays brings summer.

Both the northern and southern halves of the world have the same pattern of seasons but in reverse. When the north is pointing toward the sun and enjoying summer, the south is tilted away from it and has winter.

All the planets tilt in some way. Earth, Mars, Saturn and Neptune tilt at angles of between 23 and 29 degrees. Mercury, Venus and Jupiter spin in a more upright fashion at angles of only 3 to 7 degrees from the upright. Uranus has the largest tilt of all. It spins on its side at an angle of 98 degrees.

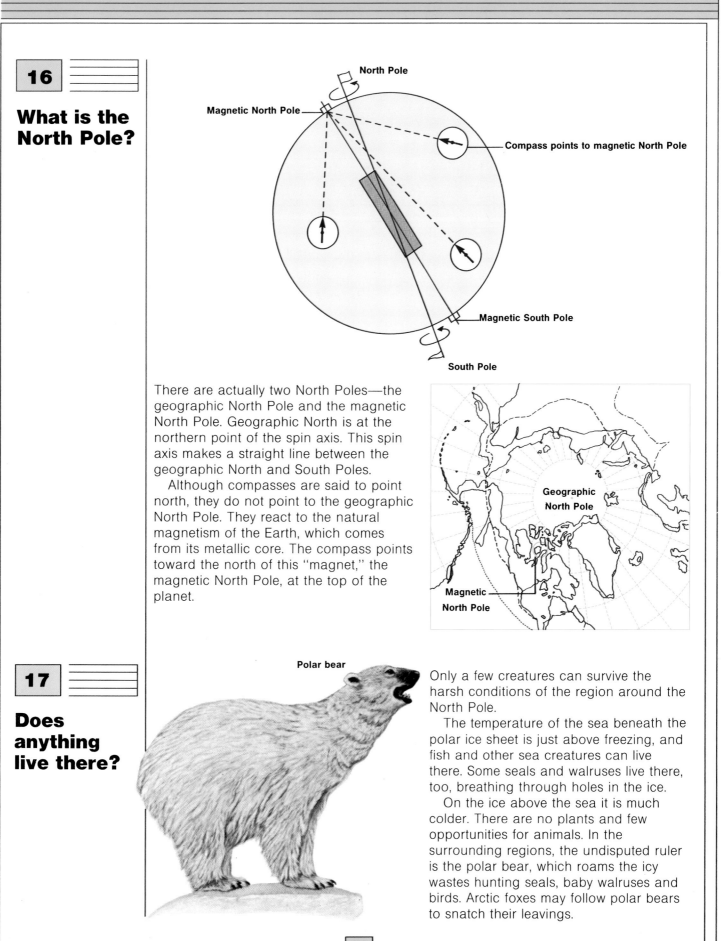

16

What is the North Pole?

North Pole

Magnetic North Pole

Compass points to magnetic North Pole

Magnetic South Pole

South Pole

There are actually two North Poles—the geographic North Pole and the magnetic North Pole. Geographic North is at the northern point of the spin axis. This spin axis makes a straight line between the geographic North and South Poles.

Although compasses are said to point north, they do not point to the geographic North Pole. They react to the natural magnetism of the Earth, which comes from its metallic core. The compass points toward the north of this "magnet," the magnetic North Pole, at the top of the planet.

Geographic North Pole

Magnetic North Pole

17

Does anything live there?

Polar bear

Only a few creatures can survive the harsh conditions of the region around the North Pole.

The temperature of the sea beneath the polar ice sheet is just above freezing, and fish and other sea creatures can live there. Some seals and walruses live there, too, breathing through holes in the ice.

On the ice above the sea it is much colder. There are no plants and few opportunities for animals. In the surrounding regions, the undisputed ruler is the polar bear, which roams the icy wastes hunting seals, baby walruses and birds. Arctic foxes may follow polar bears to snatch their leavings.

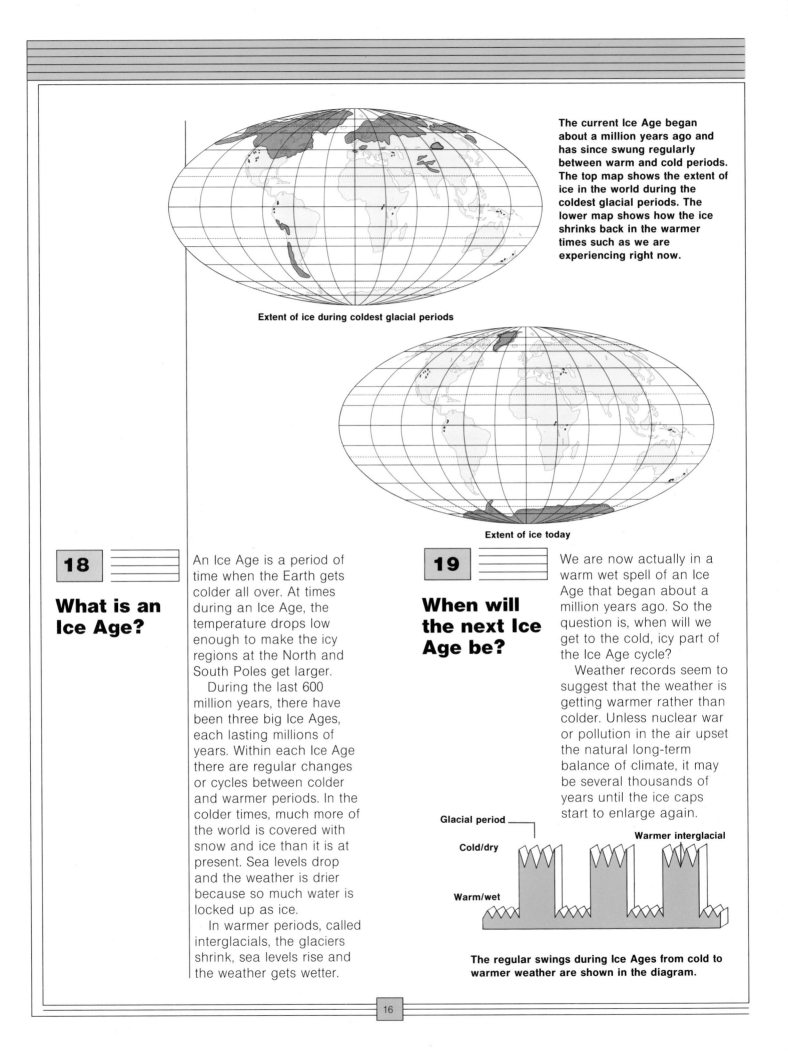

Extent of ice during coldest glacial periods

The current Ice Age began about a million years ago and has since swung regularly between warm and cold periods. The top map shows the extent of ice in the world during the coldest glacial periods. The lower map shows how the ice shrinks back in the warmer times such as we are experiencing right now.

Extent of ice today

What is an Ice Age?

An Ice Age is a period of time when the Earth gets colder all over. At times during an Ice Age, the temperature drops low enough to make the icy regions at the North and South Poles get larger.

During the last 600 million years, there have been three big Ice Ages, each lasting millions of years. Within each Ice Age there are regular changes or cycles between colder and warmer periods. In the colder times, much more of the world is covered with snow and ice than it is at present. Sea levels drop and the weather is drier because so much water is locked up as ice.

In warmer periods, called interglacials, the glaciers shrink, sea levels rise and the weather gets wetter.

When will the next Ice Age be?

We are now actually in a warm wet spell of an Ice Age that began about a million years ago. So the question is, when will we get to the cold, icy part of the Ice Age cycle?

Weather records seem to suggest that the weather is getting warmer rather than colder. Unless nuclear war or pollution in the air upset the natural long-term balance of climate, it may be several thousands of years until the ice caps start to enlarge again.

Glacial period

Cold/dry

Warmer interglacial

Warm/wet

The regular swings during Ice Ages from cold to warmer weather are shown in the diagram.

How do animals survive an Ice Age?

Animals survive the cold period of an Ice Age by moving out of reach of the ice caps or by slowly adapting to the colder conditions.

The glacial or coldest periods of Ice Ages do not come on overnight. During the lifetime of any one creature, even a long-lived animal such as an elephant, changes in climate are far too small to be noticed.

So plants and animals have plenty of time to adapt. First, as an area gets colder, the types of plant that grow there gradually change—tundra plants such as lichens and low-growing shrubs take over woodland, for example. If plant life changes, the types of animals living in the area must too. Those living there must adapt to the new conditions in order to survive, and other creatures from farther north may move into the area.

One way animals cope with Ice Age conditions is slowly to move away from the ice sheet. For instance, when northern Europe was last covered with ice 20,000 years ago, insect-eating birds such as warblers moved south to find warmer quarters around the Mediterranean area.

Other animals gradually adapted to the cold. Elephants and rhinos, for example, which we think of today as hot country creatures, managed surprisingly well. Special kinds evolved with long hairy coats to keep them warm. These woolly mammoths and rhinos flourished in the coldest times of the Ice Age.

Woolly mammoth

Woolly mammoths thrived in a cold period of the Ice Age 40,000 to 30,000 years ago, although their present-day relatives, elephants, live in tropical countries. Mammoths had thick woolly coats and plenty of body fat to protect them from the icy weather.

Why does the moon change shape?

The moon does not really change shape. It seems to, but really it is always the same ball of rock. What does change, though, is the amount of its shining surface, lit by the sun, that we can see from Earth. The lit part of the side of the moon facing us is all that we can see; the rest of that side merges with the dark nighttime sky and is invisible.

The moon shines only by reflecting light from the sun. About half of its surface is always lit by the sun's rays; the other half, facing away from the sun, is dark.

The moon always keeps the same side facing Earth. The other side was invisible until spacecrafts circled the moon and took photographs. From Earth, the amount of the visible side of the moon that is lit up changes as the moon orbits. For much of its orbit, at least some of its lit surface is on the side we cannot see. Only at the halfway stage of its orbit, when the Earth is directly between the moon and the sun, do we see the whole of the lit half—the full moon.

The way our year is divided is based on the moon's 28-day orbit—the month. But there is not an exact number of moon cycles in a year—the period of time that it takes the Earth to orbit the sun. To stop the moon-based months and the yearly cycle of seasons drifting out of step with each other, calendar months have been adjusted to slightly different lengths—28, 29, 30 and 31 days.

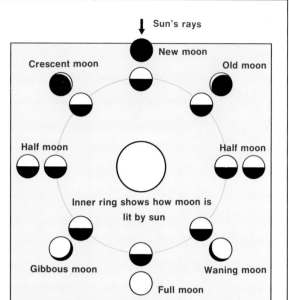

Inner ring shows how moon is lit by sun

Outer ring shows how much of lit moon is seen from Earth

The moon regularly orbits the Earth in just under 28 days. As it orbits, it keeps the same side facing Earth all the time. Half of its surface is lit by the sun, half is always dark. The amount of the lit surface we can see from Earth changes as the moon moves around the Earth.

When the moon is between Earth and the sun, we cannot see its lit side at all; the side that we never see is facing toward the sun. As the moon moves around on the path of its orbit, we see first a thin sliver of lit surface, then a wider crescent, then a half moon. At the point of the moon's orbit when Earth is between it and the sun, we see a full moon. The whole of the moon's lit surface is visible from Earth. From then on the right-hand side is more and more in shadow until, once again, the moon cannot be seen at all.

What is it like on the moon?

Almost everything about the moon is different from conditions on our own planet, Earth. Although the moon is about 238,866 miles (384,400 km) away, we know what it is like there from the visits of astronauts.

There is no air on the moon. So, to step out onto the moon at all, astronauts had to wear spacesuits equipped with breathing apparatus. Because there is no air, there is no sound—sound is carried in air. Men on the moon had to talk to each other through walkie-talkie radios, built into their helmets.

There is no water on the moon—no rivers, seas, lakes, clouds in the sky or rain. This means that nothing can live

naturally on the moon. No animals or plants have ever lived there, not even the tiniest micro-organisms. With no air or water, there is no weather. The cloudless lunar sky is always black, like the nighttime sky on Earth.

The moon's gravity—the natural force that pulls everything down toward the center of a planet or moon—is only a sixth of that on Earth. So everything weighs only one-sixth of its earthly weight. This explains why the astronauts could leap along so easily in their heavy space suits and seemed to be as strong as Superman. They were able to lift six times the weight they could manage on Earth.

The surface of the moon is made of grayish rock and fine gray dust. There are mountains, valleys and many craters. These craters are thought to have been made by meteors—pieces of rock or metal which hurtle through space—that crash landed on the moon millions of years ago.

American astronaut Buzz Aldrin walked out onto the moon on July 20, 1969. Because there is no wind or rain to disturb the dusty surface, his footprints will still be there today.

Where does the sea go when the tide goes out?

When the tide goes out, the water does not really disappear. It just moves from one place to another on the Earth's surface. The total amount of seawater in the oceans and seas of the world remains the same from hour to hour, but it is spread out differently on the Earth's surface as the tides change from high to low and back again.

Tides happen because both the moon and the sun pull the Earth's seawater

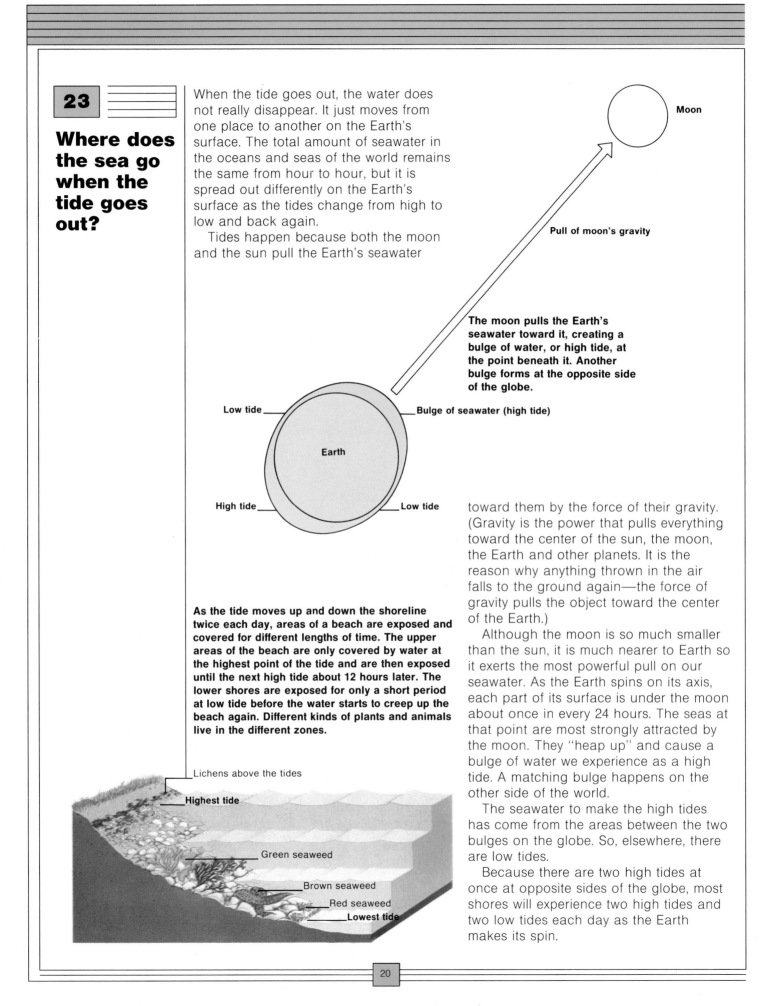

Moon

Pull of moon's gravity

The moon pulls the Earth's seawater toward it, creating a bulge of water, or high tide, at the point beneath it. Another bulge forms at the opposite side of the globe.

Low tide

Bulge of seawater (high tide)

Earth

High tide

Low tide

As the tide moves up and down the shoreline twice each day, areas of a beach are exposed and covered for different lengths of time. The upper areas of the beach are only covered by water at the highest point of the tide and are then exposed until the next high tide about 12 hours later. The lower shores are exposed for only a short period at low tide before the water starts to creep up the beach again. Different kinds of plants and animals live in the different zones.

Lichens above the tides

Highest tide

Green seaweed

Brown seaweed

Red seaweed

Lowest tide

toward them by the force of their gravity. (Gravity is the power that pulls everything toward the center of the sun, the moon, the Earth and other planets. It is the reason why anything thrown in the air falls to the ground again—the force of gravity pulls the object toward the center of the Earth.)

Although the moon is so much smaller than the sun, it is much nearer to Earth so it exerts the most powerful pull on our seawater. As the Earth spins on its axis, each part of its surface is under the moon about once in every 24 hours. The seas at that point are most strongly attracted by the moon. They "heap up" and cause a bulge of water we experience as a high tide. A matching bulge happens on the other side of the world.

The seawater to make the high tides has come from the areas between the two bulges on the globe. So, elsewhere, there are low tides.

Because there are two high tides at once at opposite sides of the globe, most shores will experience two high tides and two low tides each day as the Earth makes its spin.

24

Are there tides in all the seas of the world?

There is some movement of the tide in all the seas and oceans of the world that are not completely isolated. As long as there is a way that the seawater can move from one part of the Earth's surface to another, there will be twice-daily cycles of rising and falling tides.

The amount of movement of the tide, though, varies enormously from place to place. The greater and more open the ocean or sea the greater the tidal extremes. So, on either side of the Atlantic and Pacific, shorelines have very high high tides and very low low tides. The difference between the two can be as much as 40 feet (12 m).

Smaller seas that are almost entirely surrounded by land have much smaller tides. The Mediterranean Sea, for example, is linked with the Atlantic Ocean only by the narrow channel of the Strait of Gibraltar. The movement of seawater is extremely restricted so there is usually only a few inches difference between high and low tides.

The shape of a shoreline affects the tide, too. On a gently curving coastline there is plenty of room for the incoming tide to spread out. In a narrow bay or channel the water may "pile up" creating extremely high tides.

It is at coastlines that the effects of the movements of tides are most dramatic. On this Atlantic shore, turbulent waves crash over the rocks.

Why are some tides higher than others?

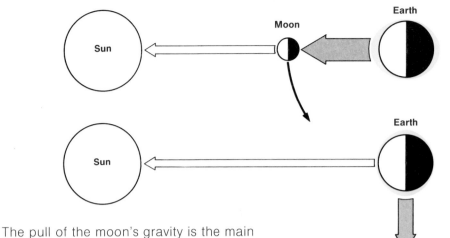

When the moon, sun and Earth are in a line, the combined pull of the sun and moon make higher than usual tides. When sun and moon are at right angles, the pull of the sun lessens the effect of the moon, making smaller tides.

The pull of the moon's gravity is the main cause of the tides on Earth, but the gravity of the sun also has an effect. The additional pull of the sun makes some high tides extremely high and some low tides very low.

The moon orbits the Earth every 28 days. Twice during its journey the sun, Earth and moon lie in a straight line: once when the moon is between the sun and the Earth, and again when the Earth is between the sun and the moon.

At these two stages in the moon's cycle, about 14 days apart, the moon, sun and Earth are in an almost straight line. The gravitational pulls of the sun and moon work together to make bigger than usual bulges in the Earth's seawater. These extra-high high tides and especially low low tides are known as the spring tides. Spring tides happen at any time of year, not just in spring.

About a week after the spring tides, the relative positions of the Earth, sun and moon have changed so that they make a right angle. The moon's pull on the water is partly offset by the pull of the sun in another direction. This results in smaller tides, the so-called neap tides, in which the high tides are not so high and the low tides not so low. Like the spring tides these come twice in every 28 days.

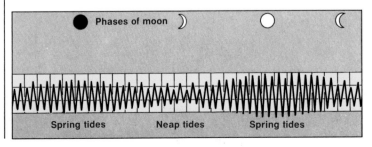

The rhythm of the tides on the Atlantic coast of the USA is shown in the diagram, left. The deeper the zigzag trace on the graph, the higher and lower the tides.

Do sea creatures go in and out with the tide?

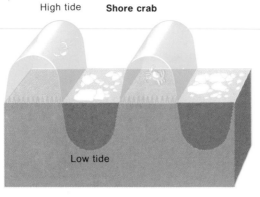

High tide   **Shore crab**   High tide   **Fiddler crab**

Low tide   Low tide

Fiddler crab

Shore crabs cannot stand too much exposure to air, which can dry out their delicate bodies. They are in tune with the tides and hide under rocks or seaweed as the tide goes out. When the tide comes in again, they emerge to find food. The crabs follow a regular rhythm and go into hiding about once every 12 hours, even if taken away from the shore.

The fiddler crab is just the opposite of the shore crab and hunts for its food while the shore is uncovered at low tide. At high tide the fiddler stays hidden in its burrow. Biological studies of the fiddler crab have shown that it has a built-in ability to measure the timing of the tides. Its "body clock" tells it when to go into hiding and its rhythm of activity continues automatically.

The fiddler crab is an example of an animal that searches for its food at low tide, when the shore is uncovered.

Some fish, jellyfish and other creatures do move in and out with the tide, so that they are always able to feed in shallow water. Others stay on a particular area of shore and manage to cope with the changing conditions.

A home on the seashore below the high tideline is exposed to air twice every day. When the tide goes out, many animals, such as razor shells, cockles and some worms, burrow into the sand to protect themselves from the wind and weather, which can dry out their delicate bodies. When the sea returns they come out and begin to feed again.

Other creatures, such as some crabs, fish and worms, hide under rocks or damp seaweed while the tide is out, or take refuge in rock pools.

Barnacles, mussels and sea anemones are all examples of animals that live attached to rocks and cannot easily move as conditions change. They open up and feed when the tide is in and covering them but close up to keep themselves from drying out when the tide is out. Depending on where on the shore it lives, each creature has its means of survival.

What are eclipses?

In an eclipse, part or all of the sun or moon is hidden from Earth's view. Eclipses happen when the Earth and moon line up in certain positions as the moon orbits the Earth and the Earth orbits the sun.

When the Earth passes between the sun and the moon, its shadow can cover the moon. This is an eclipse of the moon.

An eclipse of the sun happens when the moon passes between the sun and Earth and covers some or all of it from our view. Although the sun is so much larger than the moon, with a diameter 400 times as big, it looks much the same size from Earth because it is so much farther away. Because of this seeming similarity of size, the moon is able to cover the sun's bright disk of light, leaving only the corona, the outermost layers of its atmosphere, visible.

Each eclipse of the sun is seen only from certain parts of the Earth's surface. The next eclipse visible from the USA will be on May 10, 1994. Skywatchers in Britain and Europe must wait five more years, until August 11, 1999.

Scientists can predict eclipses because they happen at regular intervals—they have their own rhythm.

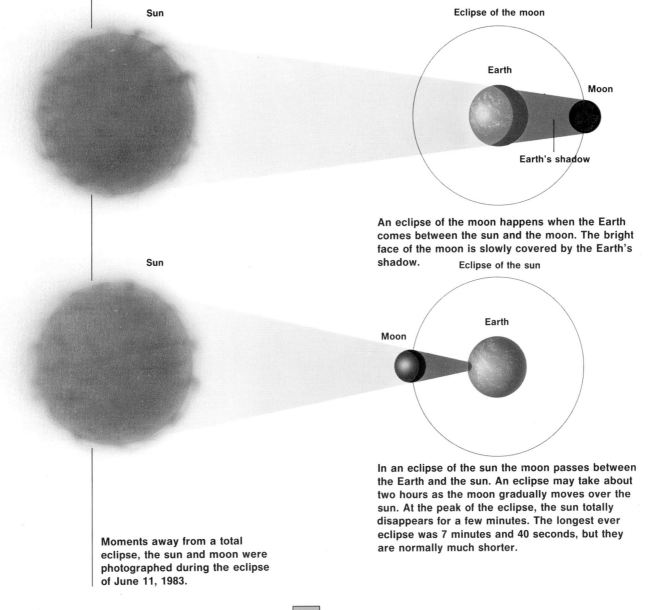

Sun

Eclipse of the moon

Earth

Moon

Earth's shadow

An eclipse of the moon happens when the Earth comes between the sun and the moon. The bright face of the moon is slowly covered by the Earth's shadow.

Sun

Eclipse of the sun

Moon

Earth

In an eclipse of the sun the moon passes between the Earth and the sun. An eclipse may take about two hours as the moon gradually moves over the sun. At the peak of the eclipse, the sun totally disappears for a few minutes. The longest ever eclipse was 7 minutes and 40 seconds, but they are normally much shorter.

Moments away from a total eclipse, the sun and moon were photographed during the eclipse of June 11, 1983.

What are comets?

Comets are balls of dust and ice traveling through space—comet experts call them "dirty snowballs." Seen from Earth, a comet is a glowing spot in the night sky, often with a luminous tail stretching from it. The comet that we know most about, Halley's comet, which was visible in 1986, is nearly 5 miles (8 km) across and 10 miles (16 km) long.

Of all the objects in our solar system, comets move farthest from the sun. But they are still ruled by the pull of the sun and make orbits around it. Some comets have orbits close to the sun which they complete in just a few years. The famous Halley's comet circles the sun once every 76 years while other comets may take several hundred years to do so. The comets with the longest orbits travel out as far as 10,000 billion miles (16,093 billion km) into space.

The orbits of comets are lop-sided: one end of the orbit is much closer to the sun than the other. It is only when comets come close to the sun that we see them. The heat and light of the sun makes the comet glow and send out gas and dust, causing the glowing tail. The tail of a comet always points away from the sun.

In 1986, the Russian spacecraft Vega and the European Giotto took the first direct pictures of the head of Halley's comet as it reached the point of its orbit nearest the sun. For the first time we were able to know what a comet looks like.

As seen by Giotto, the comet appears as an irregular "blob" shaped rather like a peanut in its shell. The surface is mostly dark, probably covered with black dust particles, but inside there is much solid ice mixed with dust. From a few gaps in the dark surface, bright jets of gas and dust shoot out into space. These form the comet's glowing tail.

The famous Halley's comet blazes across the sky, its tail streaming behind it.

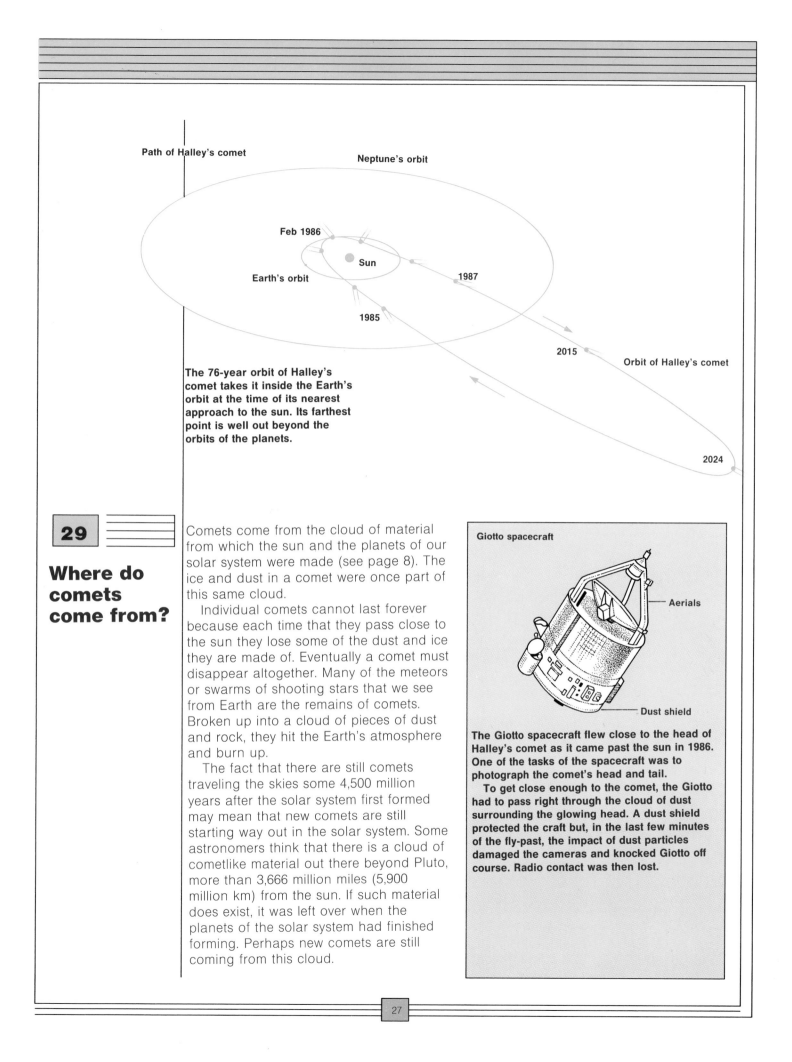

Path of Halley's comet

Neptune's orbit

Feb 1986

Sun

Earth's orbit

1987

1985

2015

Orbit of Halley's comet

2024

The 76-year orbit of Halley's comet takes it inside the Earth's orbit at the time of its nearest approach to the sun. Its farthest point is well out beyond the orbits of the planets.

29

Where do comets come from?

Comets come from the cloud of material from which the sun and the planets of our solar system were made (see page 8). The ice and dust in a comet were once part of this same cloud.

Individual comets cannot last forever because each time that they pass close to the sun they lose some of the dust and ice they are made of. Eventually a comet must disappear altogether. Many of the meteors or swarms of shooting stars that we see from Earth are the remains of comets. Broken up into a cloud of pieces of dust and rock, they hit the Earth's atmosphere and burn up.

The fact that there are still comets traveling the skies some 4,500 million years after the solar system first formed may mean that new comets are still starting way out in the solar system. Some astronomers think that there is a cloud of cometlike material out there beyond Pluto, more than 3,666 million miles (5,900 million km) from the sun. If such material does exist, it was left over when the planets of the solar system had finished forming. Perhaps new comets are still coming from this cloud.

Giotto spacecraft

Aerials

Dust shield

The Giotto spacecraft flew close to the head of Halley's comet as it came past the sun in 1986. One of the tasks of the spacecraft was to photograph the comet's head and tail.

To get close enough to the comet, the Giotto had to pass right through the cloud of dust surrounding the glowing head. A dust shield protected the craft but, in the last few minutes of the fly-past, the impact of dust particles damaged the cameras and knocked Giotto off course. Radio contact was then lost.

Why is it hot in summer and cold in winter?

The contrast between the heat of summer and cold of winter is a result of the way in which the Earth tilts as it spins. Its axis, the imaginary line passing through the Earth from the North Pole to the South Pole, and around which it spins, is at an angle. This means that the Earth spins at an angle to the path of the sun's rays.

For half of its orbit around the sun, and therefore for half the year, the northern half of the Earth is tilting toward the sun. During the period of sunward tilt the sun is higher in the sky each day and more direct light and heat reach the ground. This extra energy from the sun makes the weather hotter in that half of the world.

The rest of the year, the tilt is away from the sun. The sun is lower in the sky each day, less energy from its rays get to Earth and the weather is colder. This pattern is just the same in the southern half of the world, but in reverse. So, when it is summer in Australia it is winter in New York and London.

The temperate areas, those between the tropics and the Arctic or Antarctic zones, have the biggest seasonal changes in temperature. In the tropics the tilt makes little difference. At the Poles it is always cold but much colder in the winter when for a time the sun never appears above the horizon.

If the Earth did not tilt the temperature for any place would be the same every day of the year.

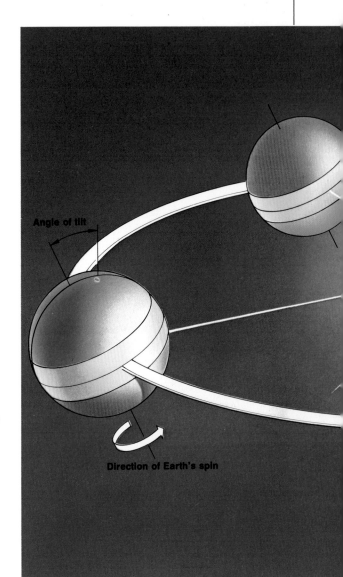

Angle of tilt

Direction of Earth's spin

Why is it always hot in Africa, cold in the Arctic?

Africa is hot and the Arctic and Antarctic always cold because of the way sunlight falls on these parts of the Earth.

A large area of Africa is in the tropics, the band of the Earth bordering each side of the equator. (The equator is an imaginary line around the middle of the globe.) In the tropics the sun is always high in the sky, so its rays fall directly to the ground, and for at least one day a year it is directly overhead. Tropical days are about 12 hours of light, 12 of darkness and do not vary much over the year. Such regular direct sunlight means a reliably hot climate year round.

Near to the North and South Poles, even during the brief summer, the sun is

In the tropics the sun's rays fall directly to the ground and bring intense heat. Farther north and south the sun's rays fall at an angle and spread over a larger area so giving less heat overall.

only just above the horizon—no higher than midwinter sun farther south—but it is there for 24 hours each day. Even so, this low sun with its slanting weak rays cannot warm the ground. In winter the sun does not rise above the horizon at all so it is dark for 24 hours each day and very cold.

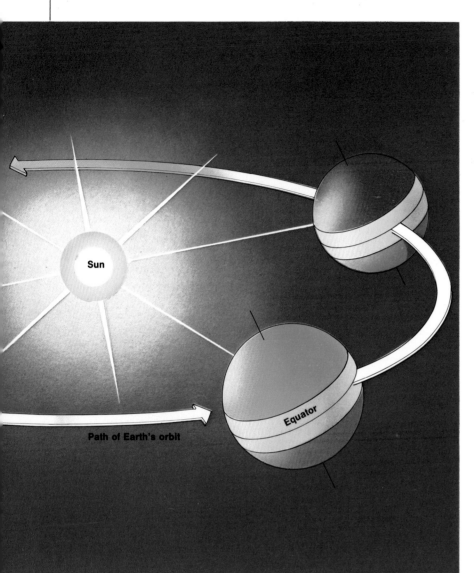

Sun

Path of Earth's orbit

Equator

The diagram shows how the seasons change as the Earth orbits the sun. Temperatures in the tropics remain much the same all year round.

33 Are there seasons in hot countries?

There are seasons in hot countries but they are marked more by changes in the amount of rain that falls than by temperature differences.

In the tropical countries bordering the equator there is a dry season and one or two wet seasons each year. All of the year's total of rain for the area will fall during these wet seasons, and plant life grows fast to take advantage of the fact that water is available.

Some parts of the tropics, though, have scarcely any seasonal change. Jungles such as the forests of the Amazon are hot and wet all year while deserts like the Sahara are always hot and dry.

32 Why does it get dark earlier in winter?

In autumn and early winter the hours of daylight get fewer and fewer. Through November and December in the northern half of the world (May and June in the south) the sun rises later and later and sets earlier and earlier. At the same time the noonday sun is a little lower in the sky each day. By midwinter day in London or New York the sun scuttles from rising to setting in about eight hours and never gets far above the horizon.

Both the short days and the low sun are brought about by the way the Earth tilts on its axis. In midwinter the northern half of the Earth is pointing as much away from the direction of the sun as it can. The rest of the Earth to the south is like a

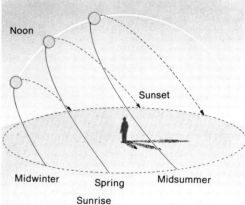

Noon

Sunset

Midwinter   Spring   Midsummer

Sunrise

huge curved hill shutting off the sun's rays through the long winter nights. The farther down the side of the hill we are, relative to the sun, the longer the time we are shielded from it, and the longer the nights.

Why are leaves green?

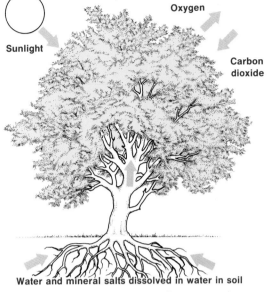

Oxygen

Sunlight

Carbon dioxide

Water and mineral salts dissolved in water in soil

Leaves are green because they contain a green coloring material, chlorophyll. But chlorophyll does more than give plants their color; it is vital to the way in which plants live and grow.

Unlike animals, plants do not eat other living things in order to make energy and grow. They can make everything they need from the simplest of materials: carbon dioxide from the air and water drawn in by their roots.

This chemical magic that happens in plants is powered by sunlight and it is the green chlorophyll that first traps that light. When the sun's rays land on a leaf some of the energy from the light excites some of the electrons within the chlorophyll contained in the leaf's cells. (Cells are the building blocks of which plants and animals are made.) This energy, trapped and passed on by the chlorophyll, helps the plant make a substance called ATP (adenosine triphosphate), which is packed with energy. It is the energy in ATP that powers almost everything that goes on in the cells of the plant.

Only when ATP has been made in the leaf through the reaction of chlorophyll to the sun's energy can photosynthesis take place. In photosynthesis the plant uses carbon dioxide from the air, taken in through tiny holes in its leaves, and water drawn up by the roots to make the substances from which the plant is built.

So chlorophyll, the green coloring in leaves, is the vital link that allows plants to use life-giving energy from the sun.

What are living things made of?

Living things are made up of cells—microscopic units of living matter. The cells are made of water and a complex mixture of organic substances, all of which contain the element carbon. Carbon is the element out of which diamonds, pencil leads (graphite) and coal are made, but it also combines with different substances to make thousands of compounds. As these compounds, carbon forms part of all living things.

Carbon constantly circulates through living things. It is passed from the air to plants, to animals and back into the air in a cyclic sequence—the carbon cycle. Plants take in carbon from the carbon dioxide in the air, and, by the process of photosynthesis, use it to make living matter such as leaves and stems. Water plants take up carbon dioxide dissolved in seas, rivers and lakes and use it in the same way.

Plant-eating animals (herbivores) take in carbon with the plants they eat and it becomes part of their bodies. Those animals may be eaten by other animals and the carbon is passed on yet again.

All living plants, animals and microbes (tiny organisms such as bacteria) also give back carbon dioxide to the air. As they "burn" sugars in their body cells to make energy, carbon dioxide is made as a by-product. The organisms breathe out the gas into the air and it is available for the plants to use again.

All living things must die sometime and the carbon in their bodies or foliage is recycled. Their remains are consumed by tiny microbes and fungi. As they "breathe," carbon dioxide is given off and returned to the air for use by plants. The cycle is never-ending.

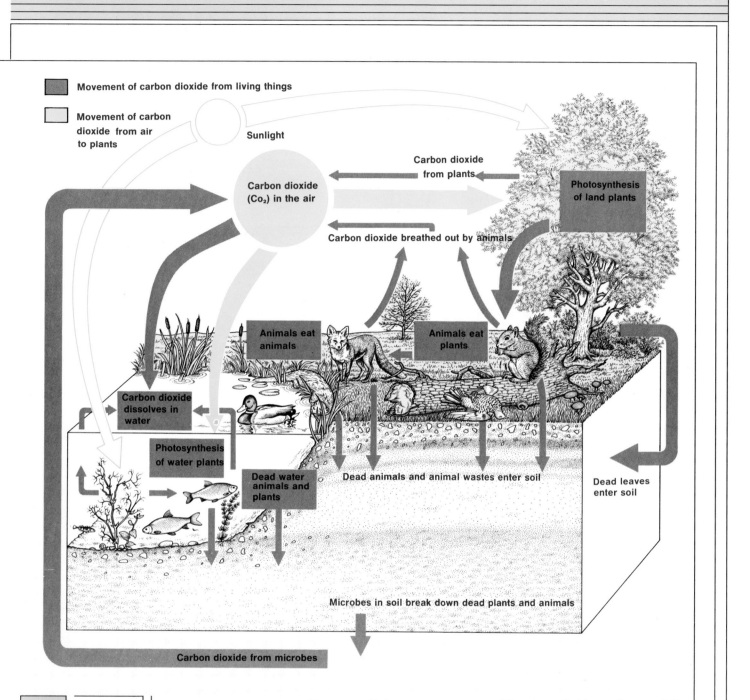

Movement of carbon dioxide from living things

Movement of carbon dioxide from air to plants

Sunlight

Carbon dioxide (Co₂) in the air

Carbon dioxide from plants

Photosynthesis of land plants

Carbon dioxide breathed out by animals

Animals eat animals

Animals eat plants

Carbon dioxide dissolves in water

Photosynthesis of water plants

Dead water animals and plants

Dead animals and animal wastes enter soil

Dead leaves enter soil

Microbes in soil break down dead plants and animals

Carbon dioxide from microbes

36

Can life exist without sunlight?

Plants could not exist without sunlight. They need its energy for photosynthesis, the complex chemical process that keeps them alive and allows them to grow. Animals cannot use the sun's energy in the same way but they all stay alive by eating either plants or other animals. However long a chain of animals eating animals may be, it always ends with an animal eating plants. So, animals depend on the sun, too, because without plants there is no food for them.

The only living things that seem to manage without sunlight are those at the very bottom of the deepest sea. No light can penetrate to these depths and some life there might survive even if there were no sun.

Specialized life at these depths centers around vents in the seabed where hot water wells up from beneath the Earth's surface. Some of the tiny organisms there, such as bacteria, can make their body substances without sunlight. These organisms are eaten by shellfish and worms which cluster near the vent.

Why do plants have flowers?

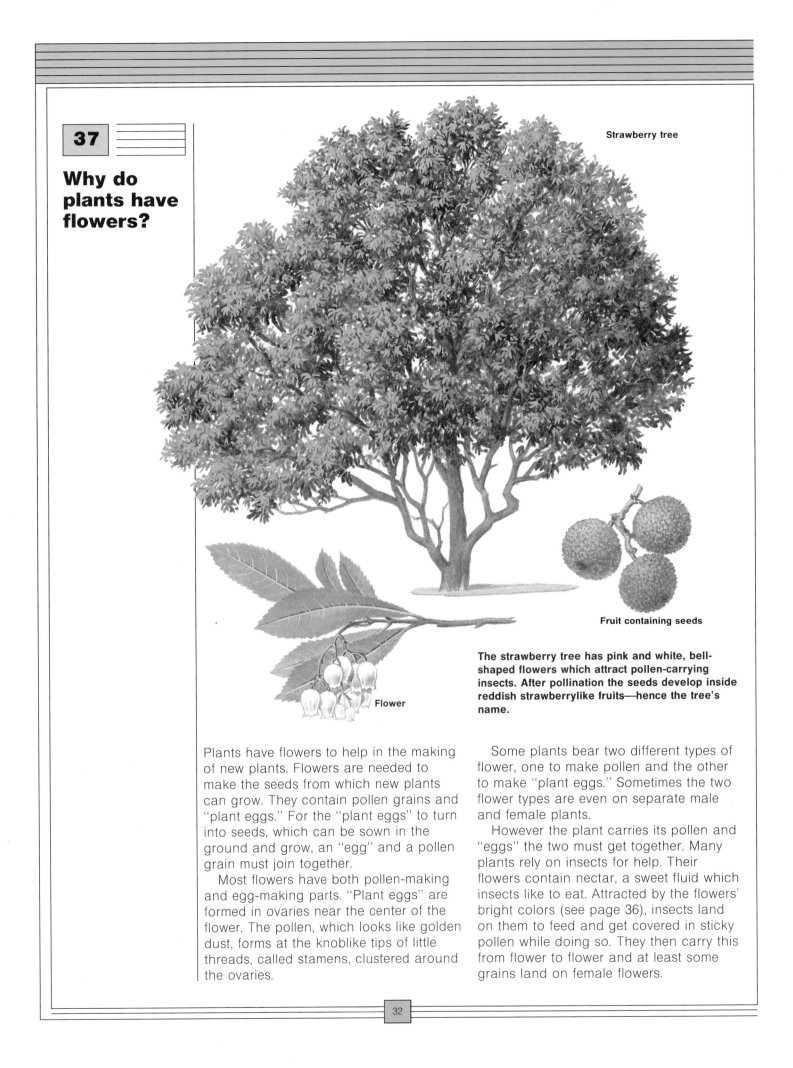

Strawberry tree

Fruit containing seeds

Flower

The strawberry tree has pink and white, bell-shaped flowers which attract pollen-carrying insects. After pollination the seeds develop inside reddish strawberrylike fruits—hence the tree's name.

Plants have flowers to help in the making of new plants. Flowers are needed to make the seeds from which new plants can grow. They contain pollen grains and "plant eggs." For the "plant eggs" to turn into seeds, which can be sown in the ground and grow, an "egg" and a pollen grain must join together.

Most flowers have both pollen-making and egg-making parts. "Plant eggs" are formed in ovaries near the center of the flower. The pollen, which looks like golden dust, forms at the knoblike tips of little threads, called stamens, clustered around the ovaries.

Some plants bear two different types of flower, one to make pollen and the other to make "plant eggs." Sometimes the two flower types are even on separate male and female plants.

However the plant carries its pollen and "eggs" the two must get together. Many plants rely on insects for help. Their flowers contain nectar, a sweet fluid which insects like to eat. Attracted by the flowers' bright colors (see page 36), insects land on them to feed and get covered in sticky pollen while doing so. They then carry this from flower to flower and at least some grains land on female flowers.

Do all plants have flowers?

Not all plants have flowers. Mosses and ferns, which grow in moist areas almost all over the world, have no flowers. Other, less familiar, flowerless plants include minute plants called algae, which grow as green slime in ditches and lakes, or a gray-green powdery substance on tree trunks. Seaweed is a bigger form of alga which never bears flowers. Mushrooms and toadstools are fungi and they, too, do not have flowers.

Some much bigger plants, such as fir trees and pines, manage to reproduce without true flowers. Instead, these plants carry their pollen and seeds in cones. Large female cones house the "eggs" while much smaller, catkinlike male cones contain pollen. Pollen, carried by the wind, joins with the "eggs" which develop inside the familiar woody cones.

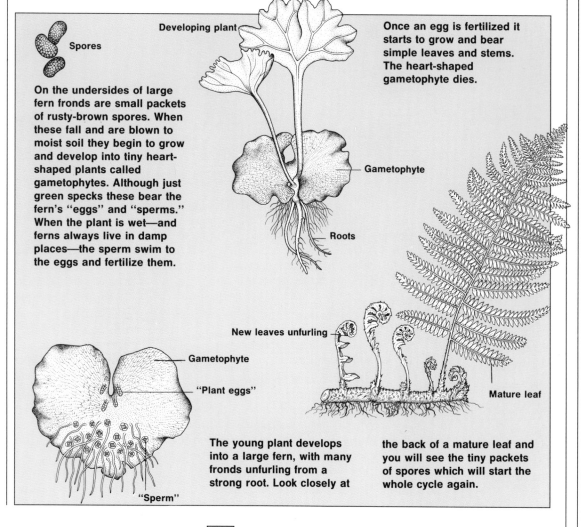

Bristlecone pine and cone

Spores

Developing plant

On the undersides of large fern fronds are small packets of rusty-brown spores. When these fall and are blown to moist soil they begin to grow and develop into tiny heart-shaped plants called gametophytes. Although just green specks these bear the fern's "eggs" and "sperms." When the plant is wet—and ferns always live in damp places—the sperm swim to the eggs and fertilize them.

Once an egg is fertilized it starts to grow and bear simple leaves and stems. The heart-shaped gametophyte dies.

Gametophyte

Roots

New leaves unfurling

Mature leaf

Gametophyte

"Plant eggs"

"Sperm"

The young plant develops into a large fern, with many fronds unfurling from a strong root. Look closely at the back of a mature leaf and you will see the tiny packets of spores which will start the whole cycle again.

Do all plants grow from seeds?

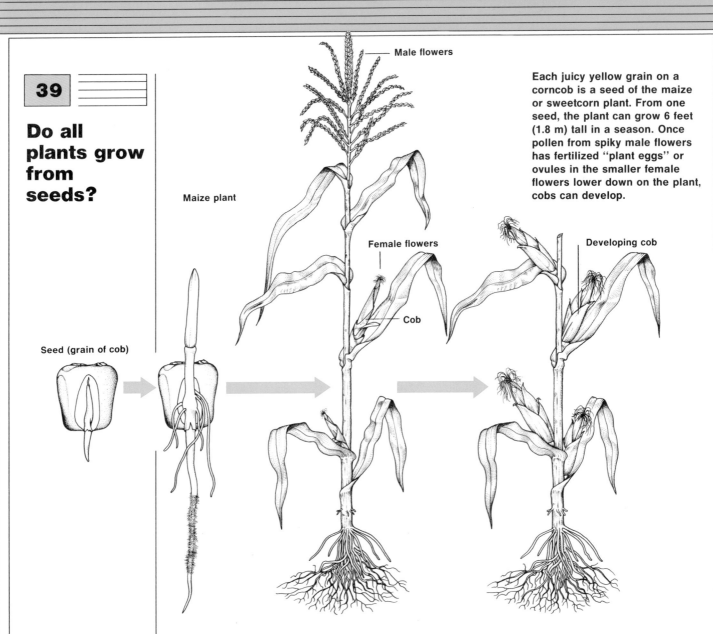

Male flowers

Maize plant

Seed (grain of cob)

Female flowers

Cob

Developing cob

Each juicy yellow grain on a corncob is a seed of the maize or sweetcorn plant. From one seed, the plant can grow 6 feet (1.8 m) tall in a season. Once pollen from spiky male flowers has fertilized "plant eggs" or ovules in the smaller female flowers lower down on the plant, cobs can develop.

Most of them do. All plants that have flowers produce seeds, and from seeds new plants can grow.

Seeds are made when pollen fertilizes an ovule or "plant egg" within the flower (see page 32). A fertilized seed is the beginning of a new plant. It has a built-in food store and a protective coat. Its job is to get carried away from the parent plant, germinate (begin to grow) and develop into a new plant with seeds of its own.

In the newly germinated seed are the beginnings of a new plant—a tiny root and stem capable of growing to form all parts of the adult plant. The seed's food store is usually in the form of one or two seed leaves (cotyledons). Grasses and cereal plants have one seed leaf; most other flowering plants have two. The fat,

protein and starch in these leaves nourish the plant's early growth when it is still too small to absorb minerals from the soil through its roots or start the process of photosynthesis (see page 30).

Some plants have other ways of reproducing themselves. Plants that grow from corms or bulbs make seeds in the normal way but also make new corms or bulbs. A crocus corm or daffodil bulb shrivels once its flowers have died, but a new one is forming.

Plants that do not have flowers—mosses, ferns, lichens, liverworts, and seaweeds—do not produce seeds. They have tiny spores which do much the same job; they blow or float away from the parent plant, germinate and grow into new plants.

How can new plants grow from cuttings?

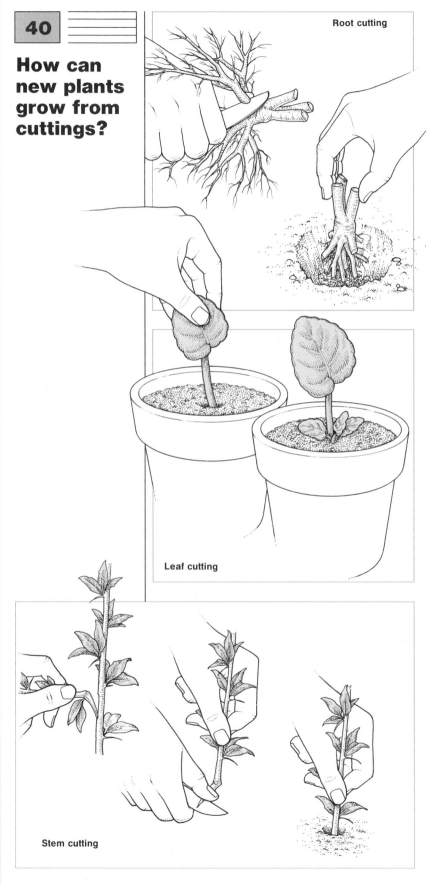

Root cutting

Leaf cutting

Stem cutting

At the tip of each shoot of a plant are groups of special cells, meristems, from which new growth comes. (Cells are the building blocks of which plants—and animals—are made.) These meristem cells are always busy dividing to create new plant material.

There are some meristem cells in other parts of the plant too, and it is these that enable a cutting to grow. For a cutting to become a new plant, it must replace the parts it has lost.

To take a stem cutting from a growing

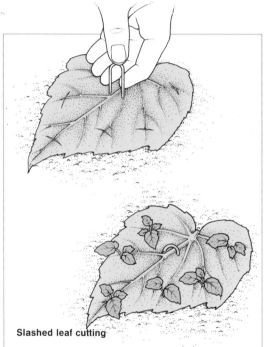

Slashed leaf cutting

plant, you cut off a section of stem bearing buds and leaves. Near the base of the cut stem will be some growing (meristematic) cells. Provided the cutting does not lose all its water too quickly and dry out, it will start new growth from these cells. A group of new cells will form around the cut and new roots will grow. As soon as the new roots are mature enough to absorb water and minerals for themselves, the cutting becomes a new and independent plant.

New plants can be grown from cuttings taken from stems and roots. In some plants, such as begonias, a new plant can even be grown from just a leaf of the parent plant.

Why are flowers so pretty?

Pretty, colorful flowers attract insects such as bees and butterflies which, without knowing it, help them in the making of new plants. For a new plant to grow, pollen grains must join with a "plant egg" or ovule. The pollen fertilizes the "egg" so that it can become a growing seed (see page 32). Insects can play a vital role in bringing pollen and "plant egg" together.

Bright petals and sweet scent advertise the fact that a flower contains nectar, a sweet sugary fluid that insects like to eat. While feeding, the insect gets covered in sticky pollen grains. If the next flower it visits should happen to be of the same type the pollen grains are able to meet and join with the "plant egg."

The colorful parts of a flower are usually the petals. They must be bright to stand out against the green foliage. The important pollinators, such as bees, wasps, butterflies and tropical birds, usually have color vision—they can tell one color from another.

Bees and birds see color in different ways. Birds, such as hummingbirds, see color much as we do. They are particularly attracted to reds and oranges.

Bees hardly see red at all but can see ultra-violet light that humans and birds cannot. Bee-pollinated flowers can be almost any color, but red is unusual. Some have markings that can only be seen by bees with their ultra-violet vision.

How do bees find flowers?

A worker bee's most important job is to gather nectar and pollen from flowers to build up food supplies in the hive.

Worker bees looking for food may travel several miles from the hive. They are strong, fast fliers, can judge time and distance well and have good eyes and color vision. Using all her senses, a worker bee can pick out a new clump of open flowers from a distance. The flowers' scent helps the bee to home in and land on them. Having sucked up nectar and packed pollen into basketlike structures on her legs, the bee returns to the hive.

When she gets back, other bees gather around her, smelling the pollen she carries. She can give them detailed information about how to find the food source she has visited by performing special dances.

If the flowers are less than 55 yards (50 m) from the hive the bee performs a round dance. She moves in small circles, first to the right, then to the left. The better the food source, the more energetic her dance. The dance tells bees "there is food nearby: go and look."

If the flowers are farther away, the bee does a more complex "waggle" dance in the form of a figure eight. The nearer the food the more turns of the dance are performed. The direction of the straight run the bee makes joining the two circles of the figure eight pinpoints the direction in which the flowers lie—see the diagrams below.

Once the other bees have got the message they are able to fly off in exactly the right direction and find the flowers quickly.

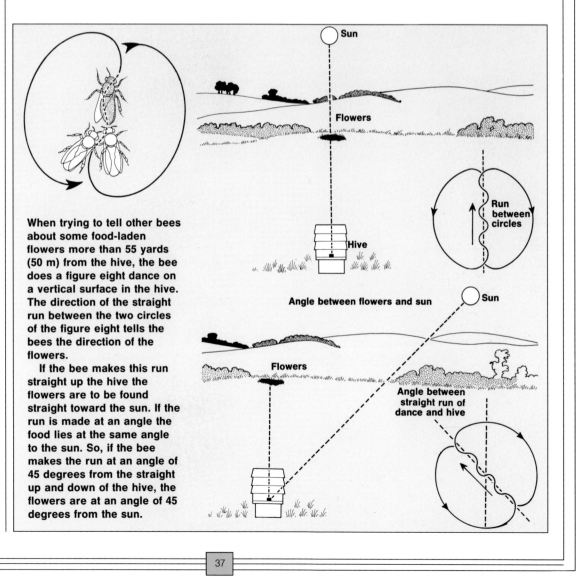

When trying to tell other bees about some food-laden flowers more than 55 yards (50 m) from the hive, the bee does a figure eight dance on a vertical surface in the hive. The direction of the straight run between the two circles of the figure eight tells the bees the direction of the flowers.

If the bee makes this run straight up the hive the flowers are to be found straight toward the sun. If the run is made at an angle the food lies at the same angle to the sun. So, if the bee makes the run at an angle of 45 degrees from the straight up and down of the hive, the flowers are at an angle of 45 degrees from the sun.

Sun

Flowers

Hive

Run between circles

Angle between flowers and sun

Sun

Flowers

Angle between straight run of dance and hive

How does a plant know when to flower?

Plants that live at least a year usually make their flowers at a particular time. Forsythia bushes flower in spring, chrysanthemums in late summer or autumn. Flowering starts off the plant's process of reproduction. It must happen at just the right time, when conditions are at their best for that particular plant and its seeds have the best chance of success.

Clearly, plants must predict the changing seasons. Their clue seems to be the changing day lengths through the year. Green leaves "sense" the changing number of daylight or nighttime hours and from them tell the time of year—more daylight hours herald spring, fewer, autumn. The plant can then switch on its process of flower-making at the correct time of year, whether spring, summer or autumn.

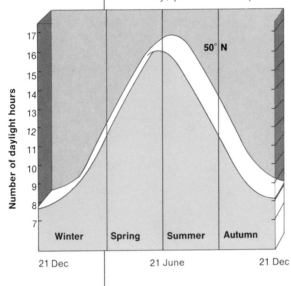

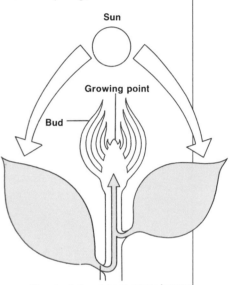

The amount of daylight in each 24 hours changes through the year. The diagram, left, shows the pattern for places on a latitude 50 degrees north—Winnipeg in Canada, Cornwall in Britain, for example. There is a summer peak of 16 hours of daylight in 24 hours and a winter low of 8 hours.

Green leaves on a plant act like aerials to "sense" daylight hours. Particular day or night lengths stimulate leaves to make chemical signals which tell the plant to produce buds, right.

Sun

Growing point

Bud

Chemical signal from green leaves

Why do daisies close at night?

This charming floral clock makes use of the fact that flowers open at different times of day. You can tell the time by seeing which flowers have opened.

Daisies, and many other flowers, close at night to keep their precious supplies of nectar and pollen from being wasted.

Flowers open so that pollination can take place (see page 36). Many plants are pollinated by insects and other creatures which unwittingly transfer their pollen when they land on blooms to feed on their sweet nectar.

A daisy is actually a collection of hundreds of tiny flowers called florets. The white "petals" are simple flowers which cannot produce seeds. At the daisy's yellow center are the true flowers, carrying pollen and ovules or "plant eggs." While the daisy is open in the sun, its white petaled florets attract insects which feed on their nectar and transfer pollen.

But at night none of the insects attracted to daisies are active. Also, nighttime dew or rain might wash away and waste valuable pollen and nectar. So, at night and even on dull, rainy days, it is sensible for a daisy to close itself up and protect the nectar and pollen at its center.

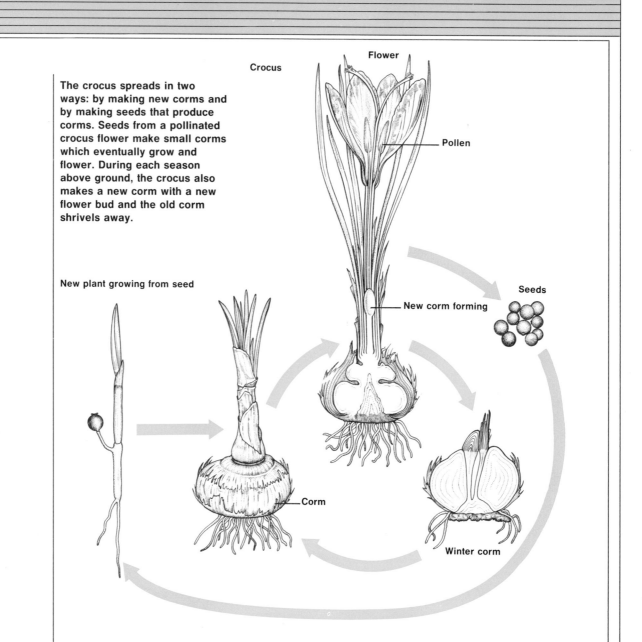

The crocus spreads in two ways: by making new corms and by making seeds that produce corms. Seeds from a pollinated crocus flower make small corms which eventually grow and flower. During each season above ground, the crocus also makes a new corm with a new flower bud and the old corm shrivels away.

Crocus

Flower

Pollen

New corm forming

Seeds

New plant growing from seed

Corm

Winter corm

How does a crocus know it's spring?

The cheerful yellow, white or purple flowers of the crocus, bursting from the cold soil, tell us that winter is finally over. The crocus grows from a corm (similar to a bulb) under the ground and hidden from daylight. But somehow it manages to push its flowers above the ground at just the right moment.

The crocus succeeds in doing this by a combination of forward planning and finely tuned timing devices, which are built into its growth cycle.

The little brown crocus corm that the gardener plants in autumn already contains a flower bud and tiny leaves. This scaled-down plant was made the previous summer when a new corm formed above a corm that had flowered.

By noting the changing day lengths, the crocus "knew" the right time to make its flower bud in the new corm.

Throughout the worst of the winter weather, the corm lies dormant and waiting below ground. Its delicate flower bud is protected from frost by the soil above it. Further growth is delayed.

In spring, the period of delay built in to its growth cycle is over and the ready-made leaves and flower begin to get bigger. The weather also has an effect—if it is very cold the crocus will be slower to restart its growth; warmth speeds it up.

So, by a combination of built-in controls and reactions to daylight changes and temperature, the crocus flowers emerge at the right time of year.

Why do trees lose their leaves in autumn?

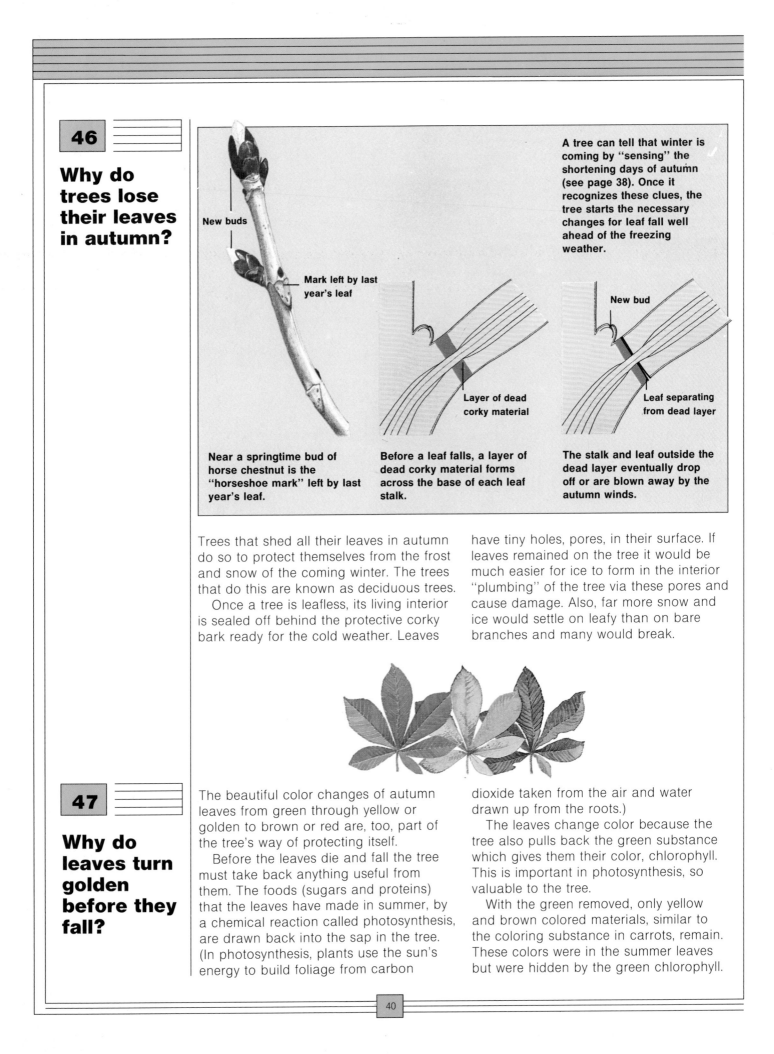

New buds

Mark left by last year's leaf

A tree can tell that winter is coming by "sensing" the shortening days of autumn (see page 38). Once it recognizes these clues, the tree starts the necessary changes for leaf fall well ahead of the freezing weather.

Layer of dead corky material

New bud

Leaf separating from dead layer

Near a springtime bud of horse chestnut is the "horseshoe mark" left by last year's leaf.

Before a leaf falls, a layer of dead corky material forms across the base of each leaf stalk.

The stalk and leaf outside the dead layer eventually drop off or are blown away by the autumn winds.

Trees that shed all their leaves in autumn do so to protect themselves from the frost and snow of the coming winter. The trees that do this are known as deciduous trees.

Once a tree is leafless, its living interior is sealed off behind the protective corky bark ready for the cold weather. Leaves have tiny holes, pores, in their surface. If leaves remained on the tree it would be much easier for ice to form in the interior "plumbing" of the tree via these pores and cause damage. Also, far more snow and ice would settle on leafy than on bare branches and many would break.

Why do leaves turn golden before they fall?

The beautiful color changes of autumn leaves from green through yellow or golden to brown or red are, too, part of the tree's way of protecting itself.

Before the leaves die and fall the tree must take back anything useful from them. The foods (sugars and proteins) that the leaves have made in summer, by a chemical reaction called photosynthesis, are drawn back into the sap in the tree. (In photosynthesis, plants use the sun's energy to build foliage from carbon dioxide taken from the air and water drawn up from the roots.)

The leaves change color because the tree also pulls back the green substance which gives them their color, chlorophyll. This is important in photosynthesis, so valuable to the tree.

With the green removed, only yellow and brown colored materials, similar to the coloring substance in carrots, remain. These colors were in the summer leaves but were hidden by the green chlorophyll.

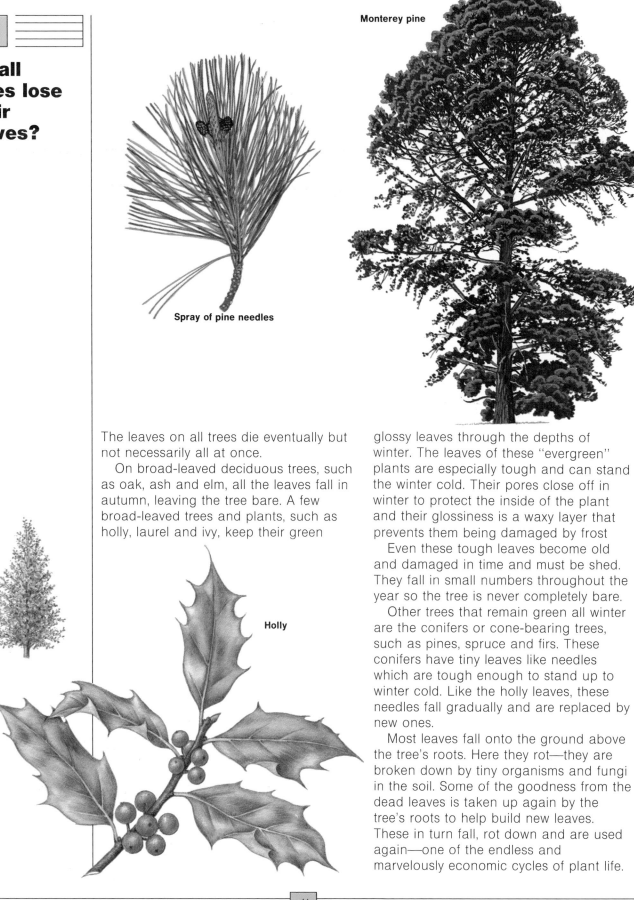

Do all trees lose their leaves?

Spray of pine needles

Monterey pine

Holly

The leaves on all trees die eventually but not necessarily all at once.

On broad-leaved deciduous trees, such as oak, ash and elm, all the leaves fall in autumn, leaving the tree bare. A few broad-leaved trees and plants, such as holly, laurel and ivy, keep their green glossy leaves through the depths of winter. The leaves of these "evergreen" plants are especially tough and can stand the winter cold. Their pores close off in winter to protect the inside of the plant and their glossiness is a waxy layer that prevents them being damaged by frost

Even these tough leaves become old and damaged in time and must be shed. They fall in small numbers throughout the year so the tree is never completely bare.

Other trees that remain green all winter are the conifers or cone-bearing trees, such as pines, spruce and firs. These conifers have tiny leaves like needles which are tough enough to stand up to winter cold. Like the holly leaves, these needles fall gradually and are replaced by new ones.

Most leaves fall onto the ground above the tree's roots. Here they rot—they are broken down by tiny organisms and fungi in the soil. Some of the goodness from the dead leaves is taken up again by the tree's roots to help build new leaves. These in turn fall, rot down and are used again—one of the endless and marvelously economic cycles of plant life.

How can you tell a tree's age?

When a tree is cut down you can see, if the cut has been straight enough, a series of rings in the wood from just inside the bark right to the center of the trunk. Each ring is made up of a double band of light and darker wood stretching right around the tree.

Each of these circular bands is exactly one year's worth of new trunk wood grown by the tree. New wood is made immediately under the bark so the newest wood is always at the outside of the trunk. The wood bands get older and older toward the center of the trunk. One double band means one year of growth. So if you count the number of rings at a point near the base of the trunk, the total will be the tree's age.

Nowadays a tree does not have to be cut down and therefore destroyed in order to count its rings. An expert can bore from the outside through to the center and take out a cylinder of wood with the complete sequence of rings. The rings can then be counted up in just the same way as on the complete trunk.

The oldest trees in the world are the slow-growing bristlecone pines in California. Some of these are over 4,000 years old, making them the oldest living things on Earth. Tree scientists have been able to age the bristlecones by counting their thousands of tightly packed rings. Some of the still-standing but dead bristlecone pines began their lives as much as 8,000 years ago.

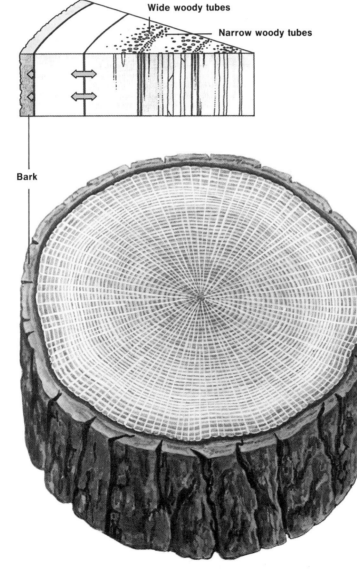

Wide woody tubes

Narrow woody tubes

Bark

Most of a tree's trunk is made of tiny woody tubes, called xylem vessels, that take water and minerals from the roots to the rest of the tree. A new layer of these tubes is always being formed just beneath the bark. In spring, growth is fast and wide tubes are made, the light part of each ring. When growth slows down, thinner tubes form, which are the dark sections of the rings.

Can you tell a tortoise's age from its shell?

Yes, unless it is very old indeed. The shell of a tortoise is made up of a number of differently shaped plates of hard bony material. The number does not increase as the soft body of the animal underneath grows, but the plates do get bigger. If they did not the tortoise would grow out of its shell!

Just like a tree trunk the shell plates grow at varying speeds during the year according to weather conditions and food supplies. As a result yearly growth rings form around each plate, and counting these rings tells you the age of the tortoise. For example, if there are ten rings, the tortoise is ten years old.

Some tortoises live to a great age—a hundred years or more—and their shells become worn and scratched. When this happens it is impossible to see the rings clearly enough to count them up accurately.

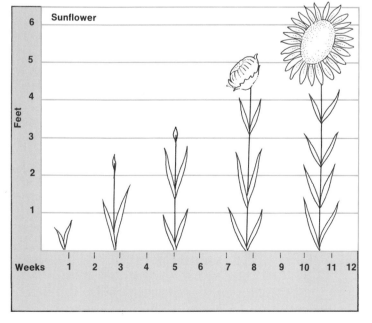

Plate of tortoise's shell

You can tell a tortoise's age by counting up the rings on its shell plates. This method is accurate in a tortoise up to the age of 20 or so, but in older animals the shell is often too worn and battered for the rings to be counted.

How fast do plants grow?

The speed at which plants grow depends on how much warmth, light and water they get. With plenty of all three, plants grow very fast. Sunflowers and maize plants can grow from tiny seeds to plants taller than a man in under six months. Climbing plants such as the Russian vine are even faster, reaching 20 feet (6 m) in six months.

All upward growth happens at the very tip of each stalk or twig. Here, at the growing points, called meristems, new cells form.

Why do caterpillars look so different from butterflies?

Although all true caterpillars turn into butterflies or moths they do not look like them because they live in a completely different way. Caterpillars crawl around, munching leaves with their strong jaws while butterflies fly from flower to flower sucking nectar through their strawlike mouths.

The butterfly starts life as an egg laid on a plant. One to three weeks after the egg is laid, a tiny caterpillar as fine as a hair emerges from its egg and starts to feed. It eats almost constantly and grows so fast that it needs to shed its skin several times as its body gets bigger. All the caterpillar's energies are directed toward growth.

When it is fully grown the caterpillar stops feeding and starts the pupa or chrysalis stage. To prepare for this it burrows into the soil or simply finds a safe spot and hangs from a little pad it spins from silk; some moth caterpillars spin complete cocoons of silk around themselves. (All caterpillars are able to spin silky threads from special sticky fluid made in their bodies.)

Once settled, the caterpillar begins its spectacular transformation into an adult butterfly, and feelers, legs and wings start to form inside the pupal case. When all is ready the pupa splits and the butterfly wriggles out to start a new stage in its life. Growth is complete. Now all the insect's energies are directed toward reproduction.

What is the difference between butterflies and moths?

Butterflies and moths belong to the same group of insects, the Lepidoptera, and there are no hard and fast differences between them.

Typically, we think of butterflies as brightly colored insects that fly in the daytime and moths as drab nighttime creatures. But many moths, such as hawkmoths, are very beautiful, and some even fly by day. And there are plenty of dull brown butterflies.

The lives of butterflies and moths are similar too. All go through the caterpillar stage before becoming winged adults. As adults, both feed mostly on flower nectar. Some also feed on tree sap and the juice of rotting fruit.

Passion flower butterfly

The beautiful passion flower butterfly lives in the Amazon jungle. It feeds on the nectar of wild cucumber plants and, unlike most butterflies, also eats the pollen of the plant. Females lay their eggs on passion flower vines.

Pupa

When the caterpillar is fully grown it becomes a motionless pupa or chrysalis. Inside the pupa case its body is transformed into that of a winged adult butterfly.

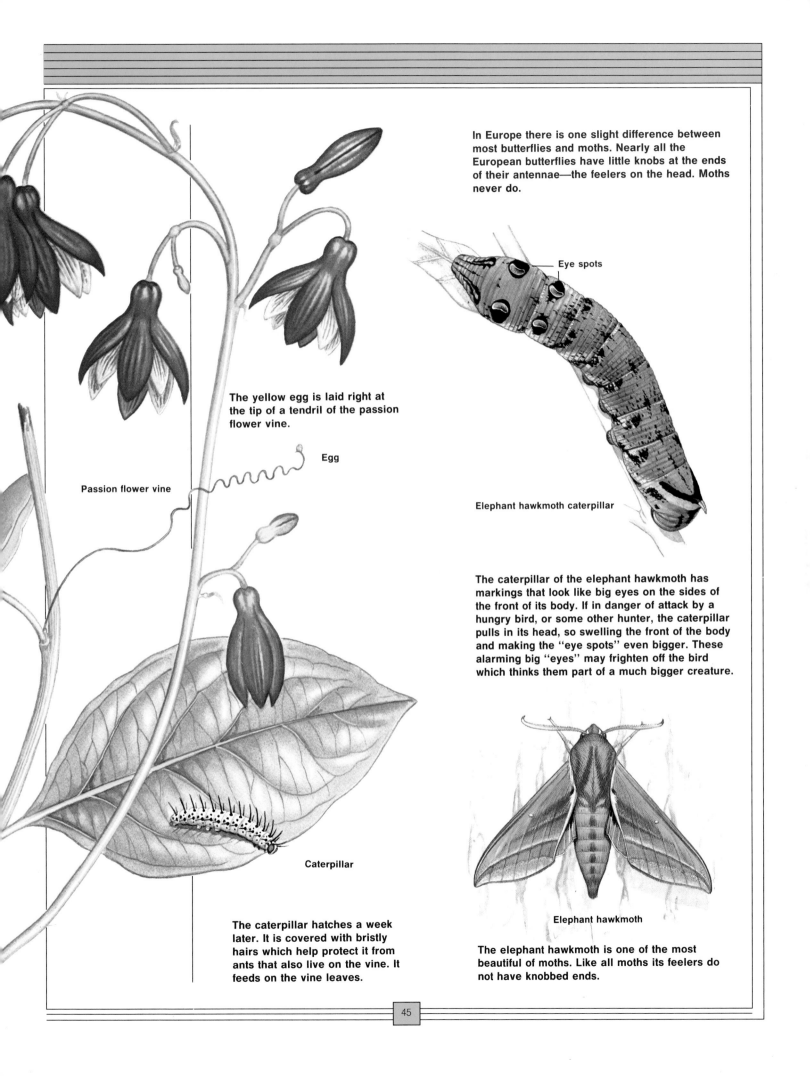

In Europe there is one slight difference between most butterflies and moths. Nearly all the European butterflies have little knobs at the ends of their antennae—the feelers on the head. Moths never do.

Eye spots

Elephant hawkmoth caterpillar

The caterpillar of the elephant hawkmoth has markings that look like big eyes on the sides of the front of its body. If in danger of attack by a hungry bird, or some other hunter, the caterpillar pulls in its head, so swelling the front of the body and making the "eye spots" even bigger. These alarming big "eyes" may frighten off the bird which thinks them part of a much bigger creature.

The yellow egg is laid right at the tip of a tendril of the passion flower vine.

Egg

Passion flower vine

Caterpillar

The caterpillar hatches a week later. It is covered with bristly hairs which help protect it from ants that also live on the vine. It feeds on the vine leaves.

Elephant hawkmoth

The elephant hawkmoth is one of the most beautiful of moths. Like all moths its feelers do not have knobbed ends.

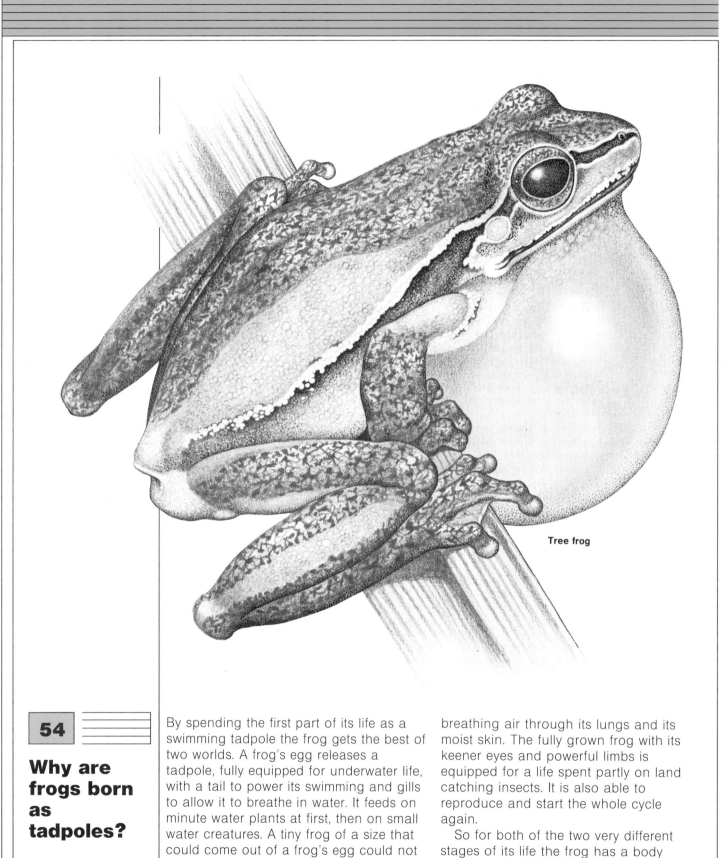

Tree frog

Why are frogs born as tadpoles?

By spending the first part of its life as a swimming tadpole the frog gets the best of two worlds. A frog's egg releases a tadpole, fully equipped for underwater life, with a tail to power its swimming and gills to allow it to breathe in water. It feeds on minute water plants at first, then on small water creatures. A tiny frog of a size that could come out of a frog's egg could not catch these creatures or swim as well. And it would be equally unsuccessful if it tried to compete with adult frogs on land.

As it grows, the tadpole gradually turns into a frog and adopts a new style of life, breathing air through its lungs and its moist skin. The fully grown frog with its keener eyes and powerful limbs is equipped for a life spent partly on land catching insects. It is also able to reproduce and start the whole cycle again.

So for both of the two very different stages of its life the frog has a body ideally suited to its activities. Because the tadpole and frog lead such different lives they are not competing with each other for space or for food. Each has its own successful lifestyle.

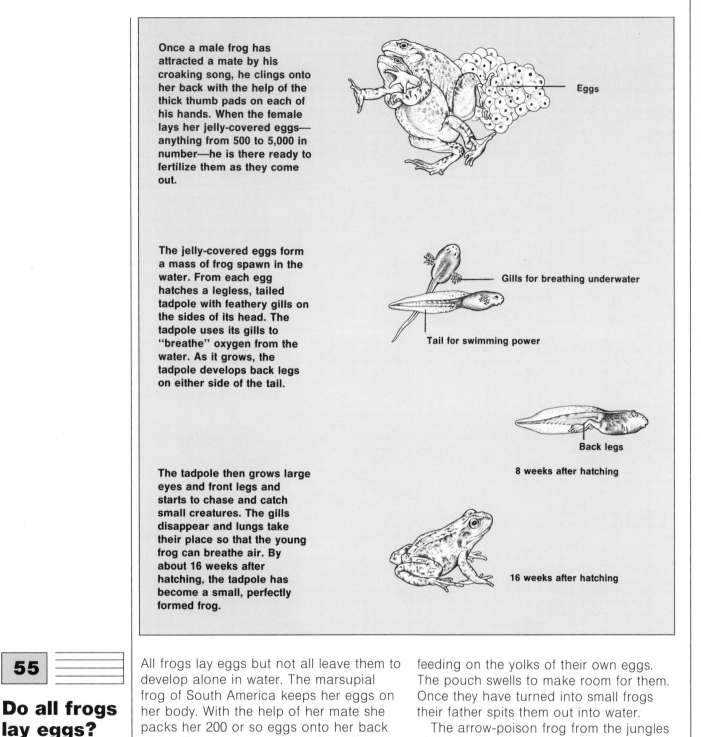

Once a male frog has attracted a mate by his croaking song, he clings onto her back with the help of the thick thumb pads on each of his hands. When the female lays her jelly-covered eggs—anything from 500 to 5,000 in number—he is there ready to fertilize them as they come out.

Eggs

The jelly-covered eggs form a mass of frog spawn in the water. From each egg hatches a legless, tailed tadpole with feathery gills on the sides of its head. The tadpole uses its gills to "breathe" oxygen from the water. As it grows, the tadpole develops back legs on either side of the tail.

Gills for breathing underwater

Tail for swimming power

Back legs

8 weeks after hatching

The tadpole then grows large eyes and front legs and starts to chase and catch small creatures. The gills disappear and lungs take their place so that the young frog can breathe air. By about 16 weeks after hatching, the tadpole has become a small, perfectly formed frog.

16 weeks after hatching

55

Do all frogs lay eggs?

All frogs lay eggs but not all leave them to develop alone in water. The marsupial frog of South America keeps her eggs on her body. With the help of her mate she packs her 200 or so eggs onto her back where they are covered over by a flap of skin. Here the young develop in safety rather like kangaroos in their mothers' pouches.

Darwin's frog has an even stranger method of caring for its young. The male takes the eggs into his mouth where they slide into the voice pouch under his chin. The tadpoles grow inside the pouch, feeding on the yolks of their own eggs. The pouch swells to make room for them. Once they have turned into small frogs their father spits them out into water.

The arrow-poison frog from the jungles of the Amazon lays her eggs in a damp place on land. Her mate guards them until they hatch into tadpoles then carries them on his back up into the trees. Here he finds a bromeliad—a plant that holds a pool of water in its cuplike rosette of leaves. He releases his tadpoles into the pool and there they remain until they have turned into frogs.

How do animals survive in winter?

In temperate areas of the world, such as Europe and much of North America, there are big differences in temperature between winter and summer. Animals which have basked in the summer sun have to face freezing temperatures, and snow and ice, in winter.

Animals need more food in winter to give them the energy to keep their bodies warm. And just when they need more food it is harder to find it. Snow and ice cover feeding grounds, plants stop growing, water turns to ice and soil is rock-hard.

Despite all the problems, animals have found ways of coping. Some simply move away—they migrate to warmer areas for the winter months and return again in spring (see page 50). Animals that make these journeys must be good swimmers, runners or fliers.

Other animals, such as ground squirrels and hedgehogs, hibernate. They sleep through the winter in safe holes, burrows or caves and avoid the really severe weather. While hibernating, the animal uses as little energy as possible so it can survive on its supplies of body fat. Its body temperature falls and its breathing and heartbeat rates are slower than usual.

Bears, badgers and raccoons also spend much of the worst of the winter sleeping in warm dens. But they are not true hibernators because their temperature and breathing rate do not change much. In the milder spells of weather these animals wake up and go out to hunt around for any food that is available.

Yet others survive the hard way, out in the winter weather. Their coats get longer and thicker and they scavenge for any food they can find. Some sheep and deer can even scrape beneath the snow to reach any available plant life.

Bighorn sheep are among the animals that keep going through the winter. They grow a thick coat and search for what food is around. Where the snow is not too deep they can graze on the sparse vegetation beneath to keep themselves alive.

Do flies die in winter?

Flies do die off in autumn and winter as the weather gets colder. But they leave their eggs behind them, and enough survive to ensure plenty of flies the following summer.

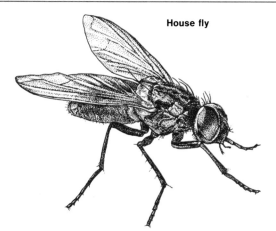

House fly

Yes, most do in countries that have severe winter weather. But although the adults die, they leave their eggs to survive through the winter. In this way they make sure that, even though they have died, there will be flies the following year.

Flies breed from late spring to autumn. They lay eggs which grow into maggots. These maggots become adult flies. As the winter draws near, nearly all of the flies lay their last eggs and die. Many of the eggs will also perish in the harsh conditions to come. But some that have been laid in well-protected spots survive until the spring.

When temperatures start to rise in the spring, the few eggs that have lasted the winter hatch. Flies reproduce extremely fast, so from these few the population soon builds up again.

Golden-mantled ground squirrel

The brown bear does not hibernate but does sleep during much of the worst of the winter. On milder days it comes out of its den to look for food.

Brown bear

The golden-mantled ground squirrel is a true hibernator. While hibernating, its body temperature falls from about 99 degrees Fahrenheit (37.2° Centigrade) to 41 degrees F (5°C) and its breathing and heart rate slow down. In this way the squirrel uses so little energy that it can survive the winter on its stores of body fat.

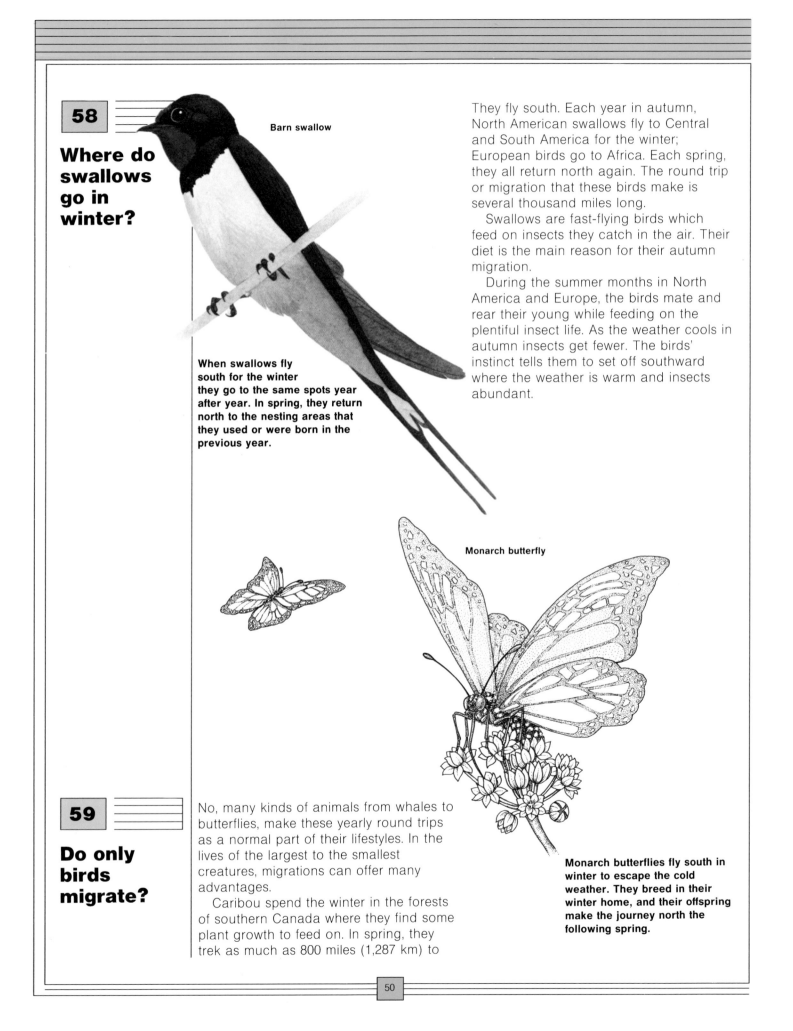

58

Where do swallows go in winter?

Barn swallow

When swallows fly south for the winter they go to the same spots year after year. In spring, they return north to the nesting areas that they used or were born in the previous year.

They fly south. Each year in autumn, North American swallows fly to Central and South America for the winter; European birds go to Africa. Each spring, they all return north again. The round trip or migration that these birds make is several thousand miles long.

Swallows are fast-flying birds which feed on insects they catch in the air. Their diet is the main reason for their autumn migration.

During the summer months in North America and Europe, the birds mate and rear their young while feeding on the plentiful insect life. As the weather cools in autumn insects get fewer. The birds' instinct tells them to set off southward where the weather is warm and insects abundant.

Monarch butterfly

59

Do only birds migrate?

No, many kinds of animals from whales to butterflies, make these yearly round trips as a normal part of their lifestyles. In the lives of the largest to the smallest creatures, migrations can offer many advantages.

Caribou spend the winter in the forests of southern Canada where they find some plant growth to feed on. In spring, they trek as much as 800 miles (1,287 km) to

Monarch butterflies fly south in winter to escape the cold weather. They breed in their winter home, and their offspring make the journey north the following spring.

the far north of Canada, lured by the lush grass and plants of the brief Arctic summer. In this way they are sure of plentiful food supplies all year round.

The monarch butterflies of North America fly south when the weather cools in autumn. They could not survive the winter cold. Instead, they spend winter in the tropics, returning year after year to the same wooded areas. The butterflies gather in huge flocks in these places until the trees look as though they are covered in living orange and black blossoms. Their offspring move northward again for the spring and summer.

Sea turtles usually make long journeys between the places where they feed and the beaches where they mate and lay their eggs. Many green turtles, for example, feed largely on sea grass and seaweed off the coasts of Brazil but travel 1,400 miles (2,253 km) to the isolated beaches of Ascension Island in the mid-Atlantic to breed. They always return to the exact beach where they themselves were hatched.

Green turtle

Green turtles travel hundreds of miles from their feeding areas to beaches where they mate and lay their eggs.

60

How far do kangaroos jump?

In a single bound an adult red kangaroo can cover 27 feet (8.1 m), nearly as far as the human world long jump record of 29 feet 2½ inches (8.9 m). Long distance, it can keep up a continuous rhythmic bouncing motion, with a hop length of at least half this maximum, for several miles.

The kangaroo's muscular back legs power its hopping movement. At low speeds of 20 miles an hour (32 km/h) or less the kangaroo moves in a leisurely way, all four feet touching the ground between bounds. With each jump, the back feet are brought forward on either side of the much smaller front legs.

When traveling at high speeds the kangaroo holds its forelimbs up clear of the ground and bounces along on its back legs. The long muscular tail is held out behind to balance the weight of the front of the body. On two legs the kangaroo can reach speeds of 35 to 40

miles an hour (56 to 64 km/h) or more.

The kangaroo's hopping movement takes much less energy than four-legged running. This efficiency is partly due to the energy-storing "springs" in the kangaroo's back legs. The springs are large stretchy tendons connecting the calf muscles at the backs of its legs to the heels. As the kangaroo lands the tendons are stretched like elastic bands by its falling weight. The stretched tendons immediately spring back again and help to thrust the kangaroo forward in its next leap.

The red kangaroo is one of the largest of the 54 or so different kinds of kangaroo. It stands up to 5¼ feet (1.6 m) tall and weighs up to 154 pounds (70 kg). Many species are much smaller—the musk rat-kangaroo is only 13 inches (33 cm) tall. The smaller kangaroos usually move on all fours and do not bound along like the "big red."

Kangaroo

61

Do spiders use all their legs when they walk?

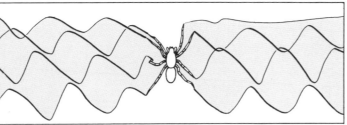

A spider can move as fast as 1.1 miles an hour (1.76 km/h) on its eight legs. To speed up, it makes each movement more often but does not change the wavelike sequence.

Yes, a spider does use all its eight legs when it moves, whether walking on a flat surface or clambering over its web. The spider's legs move in two ways: they are bent by muscles connected to the inside of each leg but stretched out again by having body fluid pumped into them.

The four pairs of legs have to be of slightly different lengths so that they do not bump into one another as they sweep backward and forward. The movements of each leg must be coordinated with those of every other in a weaving sequence or the spider might trip over itself.

Does a running horse ever have all four feet off the ground at once?

Slow motion movie film shows clearly that a galloping horse does sometimes take all its feet off the ground.

While a horse is walking it almost always has three feet on the ground. When trotting, the leg movements change to a rhythmic sequence in which two diagonally opposite feet are always on the ground together—that is, front left and right back, front right and left back and so on.

The fastest movement, the gallop, is the most complex. At different parts of the cycle the horse has three, two, then one foot on the ground then takes off all together. One hoof comes to the ground, then two and three and the cycle starts again.

A walking horse moves each leg in turn so that there are nearly always three feet touching ground.

The walk

A trotting horse lifts diagonally opposite legs together so that there are always two feet on the ground.

The trot

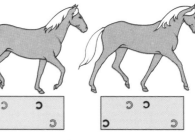

The gallop

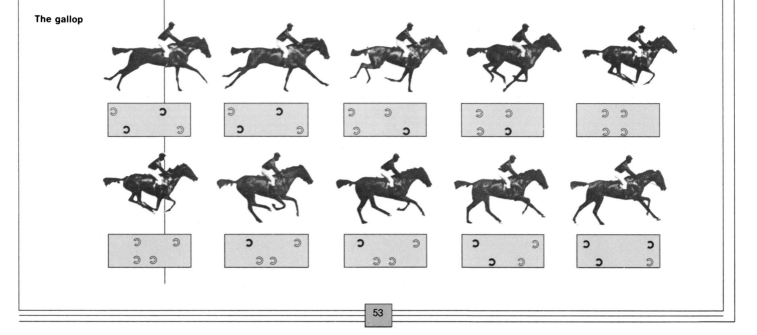

63

How does a starfish walk with five arms?

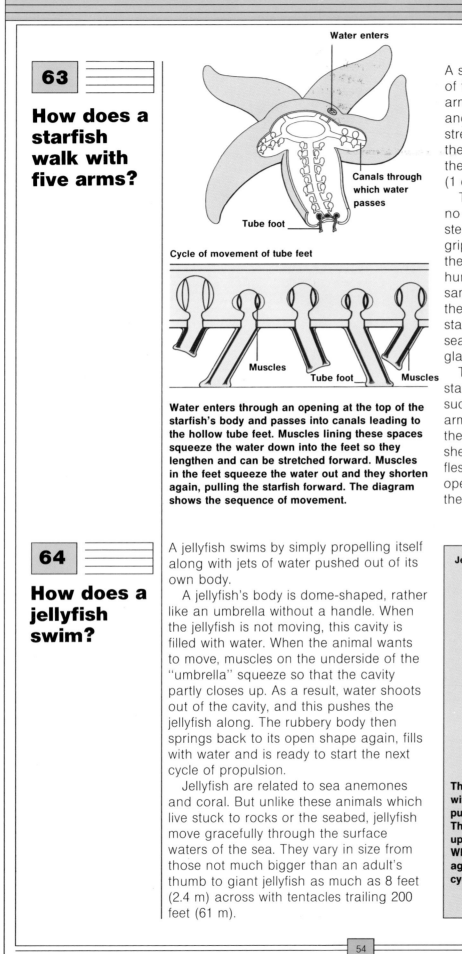

Water enters

Canals through which water passes

Tube foot

Cycle of movement of tube feet

Muscles

Tube foot

Muscles

Water enters through an opening at the top of the starfish's body and passes into canals leading to the hollow tube feet. Muscles lining these spaces squeeze the water down into the feet so they lengthen and can be stretched forward. Muscles in the feet squeeze the water out and they shorten again, pulling the starfish forward. The diagram shows the sequence of movement.

A starfish actually walks on the hundreds of tiny feet which line the undersides of its arms. These feet are like tiny hollow tubes, and, in fact, are called tube feet. The feet stretch forward as water is squeezed into them from the starfish's body. Each of these tube feet is less than half an inch (1 cm) long.

The starfish can move in any direction; no particular arm leads. Working to a steady rhythm, the tube feet stretch out, grip hold of the surface with suckers on their base and shorten again. Since hundreds of feet are doing this at the same time, each cycle of movement pulls the starfish forward a little. In this way, the starfish can move over rocks or the seabed or cling to any surface—even the glass sides of an aquarium.

Tube feet also come in useful when the starfish is feeding on hard-shelled prey such as oysters. The starfish wraps its arms around the oyster, grips each half of the shell with its tube feet and pulls the shell apart just enough to get at the soft flesh inside. Oyster shells are very hard to open so this shows just how powerfully the tube feet can grip.

64

How does a jellyfish swim?

A jellyfish swims by simply propelling itself along with jets of water pushed out of its own body.

A jellyfish's body is dome-shaped, rather like an umbrella without a handle. When the jellyfish is not moving, this cavity is filled with water. When the animal wants to move, muscles on the underside of the "umbrella" squeeze so that the cavity partly closes up. As a result, water shoots out of the cavity, and this pushes the jellyfish along. The rubbery body then springs back to its open shape again, fills with water and is ready to start the next cycle of propulsion.

Jellyfish are related to sea anemones and coral. But unlike these animals which live stuck to rocks or the seabed, jellyfish move gracefully through the surface waters of the sea. They vary in size from those not much bigger than an adult's thumb to giant jellyfish as much as 8 feet (2.4 m) across with tentacles trailing 200 feet (61 m).

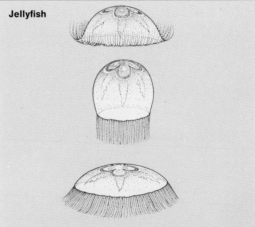

Jellyfish

The umbrella-shaped body of the jellyfish fills with water. Muscles squeeze the body so pushing a jet of water out behind the jellyfish. This jet-propels the creature forward or upward depending on which direction it faces. When the muscles relax, the body opens out again and fills with water ready for the next cycle of movement.

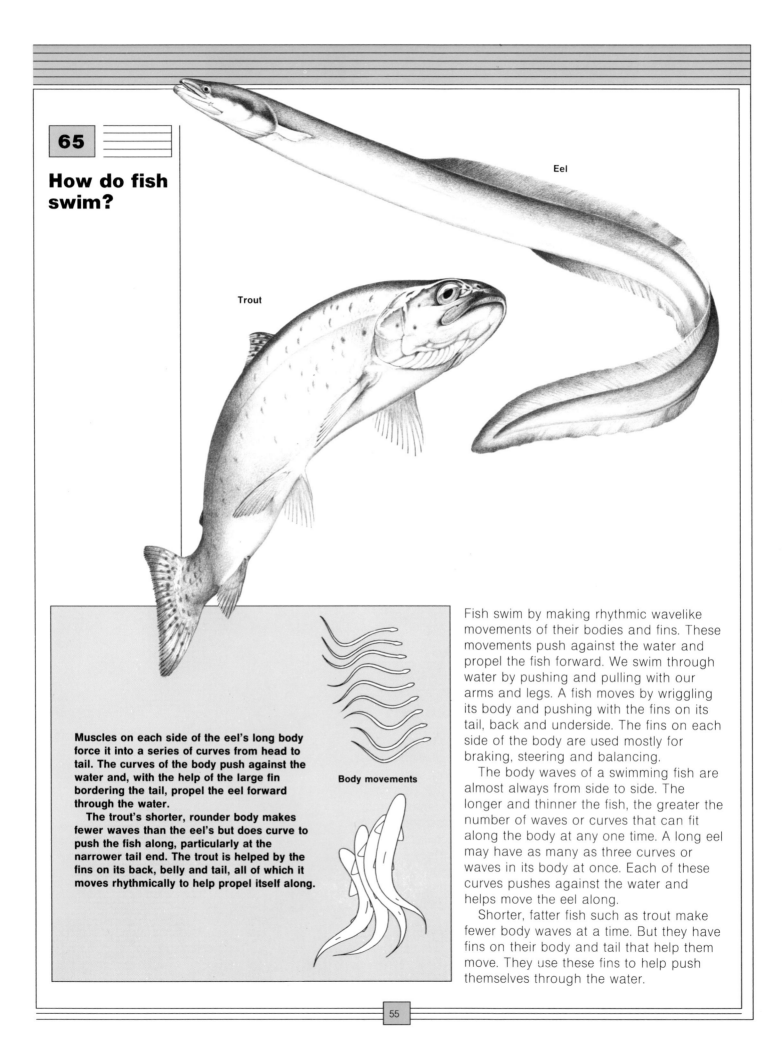

How do fish swim?

Eel

Trout

Muscles on each side of the eel's long body force it into a series of curves from head to tail. The curves of the body push against the water and, with the help of the large fin bordering the tail, propel the eel forward through the water.

The trout's shorter, rounder body makes fewer waves than the eel's but does curve to push the fish along, particularly at the narrower tail end. The trout is helped by the fins on its back, belly and tail, all of which it moves rhythmically to help propel itself along.

Body movements

Fish swim by making rhythmic wavelike movements of their bodies and fins. These movements push against the water and propel the fish forward. We swim through water by pushing and pulling with our arms and legs. A fish moves by wriggling its body and pushing with the fins on its tail, back and underside. The fins on each side of the body are used mostly for braking, steering and balancing.

The body waves of a swimming fish are almost always from side to side. The longer and thinner the fish, the greater the number of waves or curves that can fit along the body at any one time. A long eel may have as many as three curves or waves in its body at once. Each of these curves pushes against the water and helps move the eel along.

Shorter, fatter fish such as trout make fewer body waves at a time. But they have fins on their body and tail that help them move. They use these fins to help push themselves through the water.

66

Do animals dance?

Animals may often look as though they are dancing. They make rhythmical and repeated movements of their bodies which in humans would be called dancing.

Dance is one of the most rhythmical of all activities, performed by people all over the world. Dances may be formal and organized, they may happen at particular times of year or at special events in someone's life—wedding dances, for example. Dancing is also just fun.

Dancing animals may not have the same feelings about their dances that we have, or the same reasons for performing them. Generally, if an animal dances it is part of the instinctive behavior patterns between courting males and females.

Animal dances are really displays to attract the attention of the opposite sex. Once a mate has been attracted, the

dance may change into a dance for two partners. These paired dances also serve to get both animals "in the mood" for mating.

The male queen butterfly, for example, performs a fluttering dance just in front of a female. His movements make her notice him but also fan an attractive and exciting perfume, a pheromone, from his tail over in her direction.

Many birds make dancelike displays on the ground, in the air or even on water. Bowerbirds build decorated structures of twigs and flowers which they dance in front of to attract female birds. Lapwings are among the many birds that perform tumbling courtship flights, and great crested grebes have a complex ritual of dancelike movements, mostly performed on water.

Queen butterfly

In the fluttering dance of the queen butterfly, a stimulating odor or pheromone given off by the male reaches the female and encourages her to settle. After mating the dance continues as a twosome as the pair fly off together.

Male black grouse perform aggressive display "dances" at the start of their breeding season. They gather at traditional spots and, with bodies hunched, wings held out and tails spread, they strut around in front of female grouse. The best dancers mate with many females.

Black grouse

Crowned crane

Birds that perform display dances often have striking feathers which are shown off by their movements and increase the impact of the dance.

The African crowned crane has contrasting wing feathers, a "crown" of stiff golden feathers on its head and colored wattles of skin dangling under its beak. During the leaping, jumping display dance, the birds strut about, bowing their decorative heads and springing into the air with wings spread. All of these actions draw more attention to the birds' beautiful plumage.

Why do bees buzz?

The bees' buzz is the result of their rhythmic method of movement. Bees' wings beat up and down so fast as they fly that they make a sound we hear as a buzz. The wings are powered by muscle movements and beat about 250 times a second.

Bees use their buzz as a warning signal. Other animals soon find out that buzzing bees can sting and learn to avoid them. The buzzing of angry bees protecting their hive and their stores of honey can frighten off much larger animals—including humans!

The bee's wings are joined to its tough, outer skeleton behind the head. Muscles work to bend the skeleton, so moving the wings in one direction. The flexible skeleton then clicks back, moving the wings in the opposite direction.

The mosquito's wings beat about 600 times a second. The wing movements are so fast that the sound they make is heard as a constant hum.

Mosquito

Why do mosquitoes hum?

It is the rapidly beating wings of the mosquito that give off a humming sound as the insect flies. The two wings of this common biting fly beat much faster than those of a bee—about 600 beats a second. This faster rhythm means that the sound of the moving wings is heard as a hum or whine rather than a buzz.

Like bees, mosquitoes use their wing noise as a useful signal, this time connected with their breeding habits. At particular times of day, male mosquitoes form courtship swarms, usually in a patch of sunlight. The humming, dancing collection of mosquitoes flies up and down in a cloud.

Female mosquitoes are attracted to the swarm and fly into it. The pitch of the hum made by their wingbeats is different from that of males, and males recognize and are attracted to the sound. They home in on humming females, grasp them and mate.

A male grasshopper intent on courtship positions himself in a suitable spot and begins to sing. Each movement of his long back legs takes the rasping patches or files on the legs past the ridges on the wings and makes a chirp of the song.

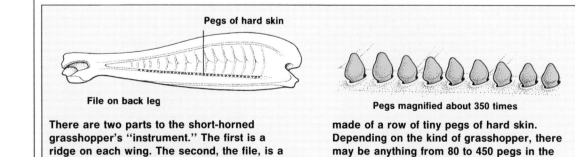

"Ear"

Short-horned grasshopper

Movements of back leg

How does a grass-hopper sing?

The short-horned grasshopper "sings" with the help of its back legs and wings—not with its mouth. Only males sing, and they do so to attract mates. Long-horned grasshoppers and bush crickets sing in a different way by rubbing their wings together.

The chirruping song of grasshoppers is one of the most familiar sounds of a hot summer day in the country. But this is a song produced in a novel way. On the inside of each of the male's hind legs is a rough patch of hard skin. The leg is moved up and down so that this patch rasps against a ridgelike section on each wing, so producing the simple repetitive song.

Although so simple, the song of each different sort or species of grasshopper has its own particular pitch and sound pattern. Half a dozen species may be singing together in one field, but females can home in on the song of their own kind.

The female short-horned grasshopper has unusual ears designed for picking up the songs of the male. The ears look like a pair of tiny tambourines, one on each side of the front of her abdomen. The song makes the surface of these ears vibrate, so stimulating sensitive nerves on the inside of the "tambourines." These nerves send messages to the grasshopper's brain to tell her that a male is singing.

Pegs of hard skin

File on back leg

Pegs magnified about 350 times

There are two parts to the short-horned grasshopper's "instrument." The first is a ridge on each wing. The second, the file, is a rough patch on the inside of each back leg which is rubbed against the ridge on the wing. A close-up view of the file shows that it is

made of a row of tiny pegs of hard skin. Depending on the kind of grasshopper, there may be anything from 80 to 450 pegs in the row. Their spacing and number help to decide the particular sound that each grasshopper species makes when it sings.

70

Do seals and sea lions have their babies at sea?

Seals and sea lions spend most of their lives at sea but do come onto land to give birth. At the start of the breeding season these powerful sea mammals gather on safe beaches, rocks or even ice floes to have young and mate again.

Seals and sea lions are perfectly shaped for swimming and diving and catch all their food at sea. But they are descended from land animals, and this still shows in the fact that they cannot give birth in water. So, their lives are a repeating cycle of movements between land and sea.

At breeding time groups of animals come up onto the beach, using the same stretch of shore or rocks year after year. The females give birth and feed their young on their rich milk. This milk is so high in fat that the young animals grow fast and are soon ready to cope with life in the sea.

A large male sea lion gathers his females together on a breeding beach. Some have already had their cubs.

Southern sea lions

Male

Where are whales and dolphins born?

Like seals, whales and dolphins are descended from land mammals, but they have become so perfectly suited to life in water that they even give birth there. They spend all their lives at sea and never come to land. But, although they may look like fish, whales and dolphins are still air-breathing mammals and must regularly come to the surface to breathe.

Because it must surface and take its first breath without delay, a whale or dolphin must be born fast. It must also be born tail first. If, like most mammals, it came out headfirst, it might drown by breathing water into its lungs while waiting for the rest of its body to be born.

Once the baby is born, and the cord connecting it to the mother is broken, it is helped to the surface by the mother and other females. Here the baby takes its first breath. The mother feeds her young on rich milk which has a fat content of more than 40 percent. (Human milk has just 2 percent fat.) The young grow quickly on this nourishing food and can start to find some food for themselves by the time they are about six months old. They are not usually weaned completely until about 18 months.

A dolphin is born tail first under water, its fins folded neatly back out of the way. The mother, often helped by other female dolphins, then pushes it up to the surface of the water where it takes its first breath.

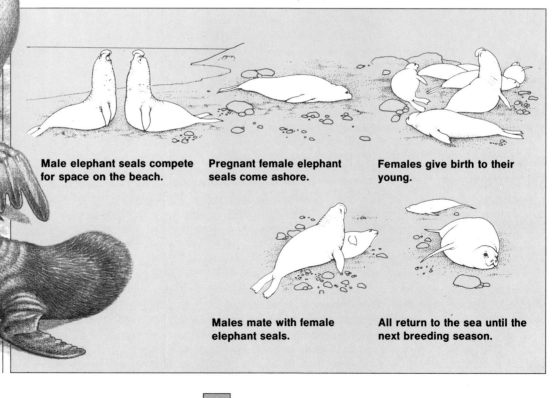

Male elephant seals compete for space on the beach.

Pregnant female elephant seals come ashore.

Females give birth to their young.

Males mate with female elephant seals.

All return to the sea until the next breeding season.

Why do birds sing more in spring?

Songbirds such as blackbirds, warblers and finches sing more in spring because for most it is their breeding season. At the start of the season, each male must set up his own territory—space where he and his mate can have their nest and rear young. He sings to let other males know he is there and will fight if need be to defend his chosen area. His songs also attract female birds.

The male bird starts all this activity as the days begin to lengthen in early spring. His body senses the change and as a result his sex organs increase in size. They produce a chemical in his body—the sex hormone—which seems to trigger the spring burst of song.

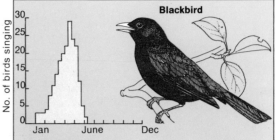

Starting in January the number of blackbirds singing in the dawn chorus rises steadily through the spring. Song peaks in May, the beginning of the nesting period. In the diagram, numbers of blackbirds singing in an area are plotted against time to show the yearly cycle of song.

The lengthening days of spring are a signal for birds to make preparations for nesting and egg laying.

How do birds know when to lay their eggs?

The lengthening of daylight hours in late winter and early spring seems to be the cue for female birds to start getting ready for nesting. No one quite understands how the change in daylength affects the birds, but it certainly sets off the chain of events leading to egg laying and so decides the timing.

In spring, as the hours of daylight increase and temperatures rise, the bird's sex organs get much bigger. The enlarged ovary (the female's egg-producing organ) makes sex hormones, chemical messengers which circulate in her blood and stimulate her to start her breeding behavior. At this time, for example, she welcomes the advances of a courting male while at other times of year she would attack another bird, male or female, that came too close.

Soon after mating, the eggs pass out of the female's ovary and are fertilized by the male's sperm. As each egg passes through the female's body, the layers of white, membrane and, finally, the shell build up. The time from release of the egg from the ovary to laying can be less than 30 hours.

In temperate areas like Europe and much of North America spring is the ideal time for birds to lay eggs. The chicks have the warm summer months in which to grow and gain strength before harsher weather returns.

Are all young animals born in spring?

No—in most mammals, warm-blooded animals such as monkeys, rabbits and bears, young are are born at whatever time of year food supplies and weather conditions are at their best. For many this is spring. For others, such as tropical animals, the best time may be after the rainy season when plant life is plentiful.

The time a young mammal spends developing inside its mother's body is the gestation period. Its length varies from animal to animal. Mating has to be timed so that this gestation period ends at the ideal birth season. In large mammals gestations are generally long—336 days for horses, 284 for cows, 270 for gorillas. Small mammals have much shorter gestation times—16 days for hamsters, 25 for mice and 31 for rabbits. These animals can breed several times a year.

Within the correct season mating can only happen when the female is "on heat," receptive to the male's advances. These "heat periods" are part of the female's estrous or sexual cycle, a repeating cycle of changes in her reproductive organs which prepares her to bear young.

Gorilla

A female gorilla suckles her young. Gorillas have one baby at a time and care for them for several years.

Are a deer's antlers alive?

Yes, when newly grown, antlers are living bone covered with skin. At a particular time each year, though, the blood supply to the antlers ceases and the antlers are shed. They are then regrown the following year.

Antlers grow out from the bones of the skull and mark out male deer in the herd. Males use their antlers in fights with each other at the start of the breeding season when they are competing for females to mate with.

The pattern of growth, shedding and regrowth of antlers is a clear yearly rhythm. In most deer, antlers are shed in late winter or early spring. By the following summer, new antlers have grown and are almost ready for the battles of the rutting (mating) season. The antlers grow under a covering of densely furred skin called velvet, but before the rutting season this must come off. The velvet sheds naturally and hangs from the antlers in untidy strands. Deer often hurry the process up by rubbing their antlers against tree branches and rocks.

When the breeding season is over, muscles squeeze off the blood supply to the antlers. The once-living antlers then die and eventually fall off. The whole cycle then starts again.

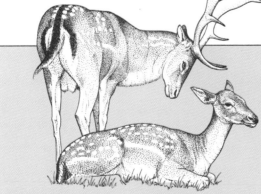

A magnificent "12-pointer" stag has six points on each antler. A male has such impressive headgear only after the annual cycle of growing and losing the antlers has been going on for several years. Each year, the antlers become a little longer and more branched.

The larger a stag's antlers the more likely he is to win his contests with other male deer. The stags start their battle by barking and roaring at one another from a distance. They then approach, lock antlers and try to push each other backward. The battle may look ferocious, with the mighty antlers crashing together, but it is rare for deer to be seriously injured.

The cycle of shedding and growth of the antlers of oriental sika deer is shown in the diagram below. The annual cycle is partly controlled by a natural rhythm built into the deer's body.

The most important trigger, though, is the way in which day lengths change through the seasons. The deer's body senses the changes and "switches on" the correct part of the cycle. In the sika deer, the antlers are regrowing from midsummer onward, when the number of daylight hours is on the decrease. The antlers are shed in late winter or early spring, when the number of daylight hours is rising.

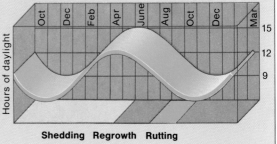

Shedding Regrowth Rutting

Do animals have winter coats?

Summer coat

Stoat/Ermine

Winter coat

Some animals really do put on winter coats—they change their fur for the winter months. Such animals usually live in cold areas where there may be snow for much of the winter.

There are two ways in which animals change their fur for winter. In some, the color of the fur changes from dark to white to make them less noticeable against the white snow. Most Arctic foxes and stoats or ermines change from brown to white in winter. Their white camouflage helps them hide while hunting their prey in the snow.

Other creatures just grow much thicker coats to protect them against the bitter cold. Bactrian camels, for example, grow extremely thick coats to keep them warm in the freezing Mongolian winter.

Most mammal fur contains two types of hair. There is an underlayer of thin strands of closely packed hair that keeps the animal warm. Projecting through this layer are longer, thicker, often colored, hairs, called guard hairs. These give the coat its color, its shape and its glossy surface.

The shortening days of the winter are the signal for animals to start growing their winter coats. First, some old hairs are molted, then new ones begin to grow.

Thicker warmer coats are made by growing more and longer hairs in the under layer of fur. Animals that change color grow new white hairs.

The lengthening days of spring tell the animals to shed their winter coats again and get ready for the warm weather of the summer months.

Bactrian camel

The bactrian camel lives in central Asia. In summer the camel's coat is so thin that the creature looks almost naked.

In winter the bactrian camel grows a thick coat that looks like a shaggy carpet.

Locust

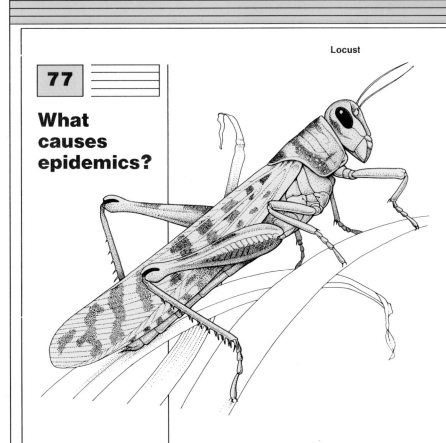

77

What causes epidemics?

An epidemic is a sudden, very large increase—a population explosion—in the numbers of a particular creature. There can be epidemics of tiny bugs or microbes, insects such as locusts, and even of larger animals such as rabbits and voles.

Epidemics are probably caused in different ways for different reasons. But in all, something that normally keeps the numbers of a population under control changes and allows that population to expand extraordinarily fast.

Epidemics are often cyclic, with predictable gaps between booms. Measles outbreaks occur yearly in the USA, every two years in Britain. Voles and lemmings increase in numbers every four years or so. Other epidemics, though, such as the plagues of locusts in Africa arrive without warning.

78

Why are rabbits so successful?

Rabbits are successful because they can breed fast when climate and food sources are favorable and increase their numbers extraordinarily quickly. They can start to produce young when only eight or nine months old and many can bear several litters of three to six babies in one breeding season.

With plenty of food around and not too many hunters to prey on the young, many of them may survive. If one rabbit has 18 babies in a season and most of those live to produce their own 9 to 18 young, just imagine how quickly numbers grow.

When one colony of rabbits gets too crowded, some individuals may move away and join another group or start up a new colony. European rabbits introduced into Australia in the nineteenth century spread in this way. Now there are millions of rabbits in Australia.

Rabbits need to reproduce quickly for they have many enemies. Foxes, dogs, hawks, owls and many other hunters prey on them, particularly on the vulnerable young. And human hunters kill millions of rabbits every year for food and to keep them from damaging valuable crops.

Rabbits

Do lemmings really commit suicide?

Lemming

No, but every four years or so their numbers increase dramatically. When this happens, the normal feeding grounds get too crowded and many lemmings try to move away. When on the move, more lemmings than usual are killed by hunters such as foxes, wolves and owls. Large numbers also die crossing rivers and lakes. Some even try to cross the sea. The increase in the number of deaths in these boom years gave people the idea that the lemmings kill themselves, but this is not so. Their deaths are accidental.

Lemmings are able to increase their numbers rapidly because they are adaptable. They are active day and night, winter and summer, feeding on grasses, low bushes, mosses and lichens. They can even feed under the snow. When food supplies and weather conditions are at their best, lemmings breed rapidly. Lemmings may have as many as eight litters, each of as many as six babies, in one breeding season.

The rabbit's secret of success is its ability to bear large numbers of young. One rabbit may produce 18 babies in a season.

Vole

Voles, like lemmings, tend to increase regularly, then decrease in numbers. Every three or four years the population reaches a peak and then gets smaller again.

One explanation for this is that as their numbers increase the voles fight more over territory. The aggressive voles which survive the battles are perhaps not the best breeders and they tend to be more prone to disease. So gradually the population gets smaller. Meeker, faster-breeding voles are left in peace to breed and numbers start to increase once more.

Another explanation is that disease affects vole populations. When the numbers have built up to a peak and voles are living crowded together, disease spreads easily. If an infection kills lots of animals the numbers quickly fall.

How long do animals take to grow up?

The time that it takes different creatures to grow up or reach maturity—the age at which they can breed—varies with the animal. It can be as little as 20 minutes. In humans it usually takes until you are twelve years old or more to be able to make a baby.

Some very tiny living things such as bacteria and amoebas (simple microscopic animals) multiply by just splitting in two. The time from one split to the next is only 20 minutes in some bacteria, three days for an amoeba.

Because they grow and mature so quickly these tiny organisms can increase their numbers extremely fast. A bacterium splitting in this way can produce a quarter of a million offspring in ten hours.

At the other end of the scale are animals that take more than ten years to grow up. Human beings, elephants and Nile crocodiles are all in this group and there is one insect that takes 17 years to reach maturity—the 17-year cicada. This cicada spends an unusually long time in the juvenile or larval stage of its life before

Bands of different time scales from minutes to years show how long it takes different kinds of animals to grow up or reach breeding age. With a few exceptions, the larger the animal the longer it takes to grow up.

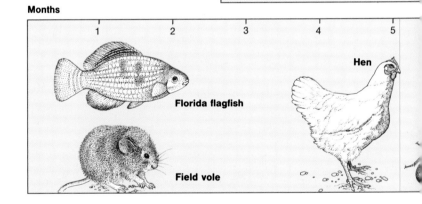

Weeks

Months

Florida flagfish

Field vole

Hen

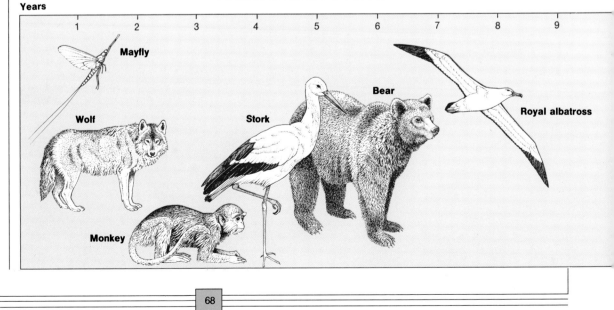

Years

Mayfly

Wolf

Monkey

Stork

Bear

Royal albatross

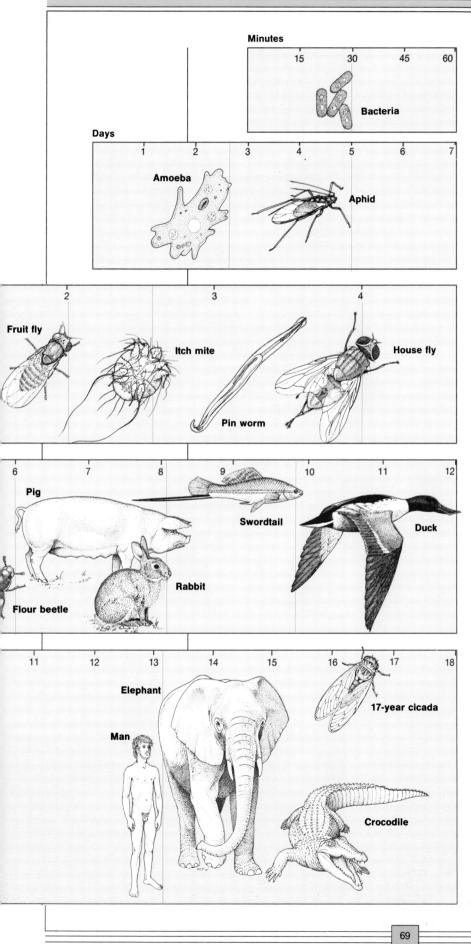

Minutes

15 30 45 60

Bacteria

Days

1 2 3 4 5 6 7

Amoeba

Aphid

2 3 4

Fruit fly

Itch mite

Pin worm

House fly

6 7 8 9 10 11 12

Pig

Swordtail

Duck

Rabbit

Flour beetle

11 12 13 14 15 16 17 18

Elephant

17-year cicada

Man

Crocodile

turning into the adult insect. Mayflies and dragonflies may also spend a year or more as nymphs or larvae before turning into winged adults (see page 70).

Whatever size they are and however long or short their lives, all animals have to cope with advantages and disadvantages in their particular lifestyle.

Small animals grow fast and being small are soon grown-up and able to bear young of their own. But they do not usually live long. Their "life plan" is to produce large numbers of young as fast as possible. In this way they can quickly take over an area, rather like weeds do in the plant world. Insects, such as flies and ants, and small mammals, such as mice and rats, are all of this type. Even though they do not grow large or live long their way of life is very successful.

Being big has obvious benefits—it is easy to frighten or ignore smaller animals if you are large. Big animals can survive cold weather more easily than small ones and can carry large reserves of food in their bodies. The costs of these benefits are that it takes an animal such as an elephant a long time to grow to that size. It takes many years for a baby to grow up and be able to bear young so the numbers of large animals tend to increase only slowly.

Large animals bear few young at a time and look after them carefully to give them the best chance of surviving. But they are long-lived so they still have several chances to breed. Most large mammals such as elephants, bears and gorillas live in this way as do the largest birds and reptiles.

There is no single best survival plan for animals. All the millions of kinds of animals have their own special ways of life.

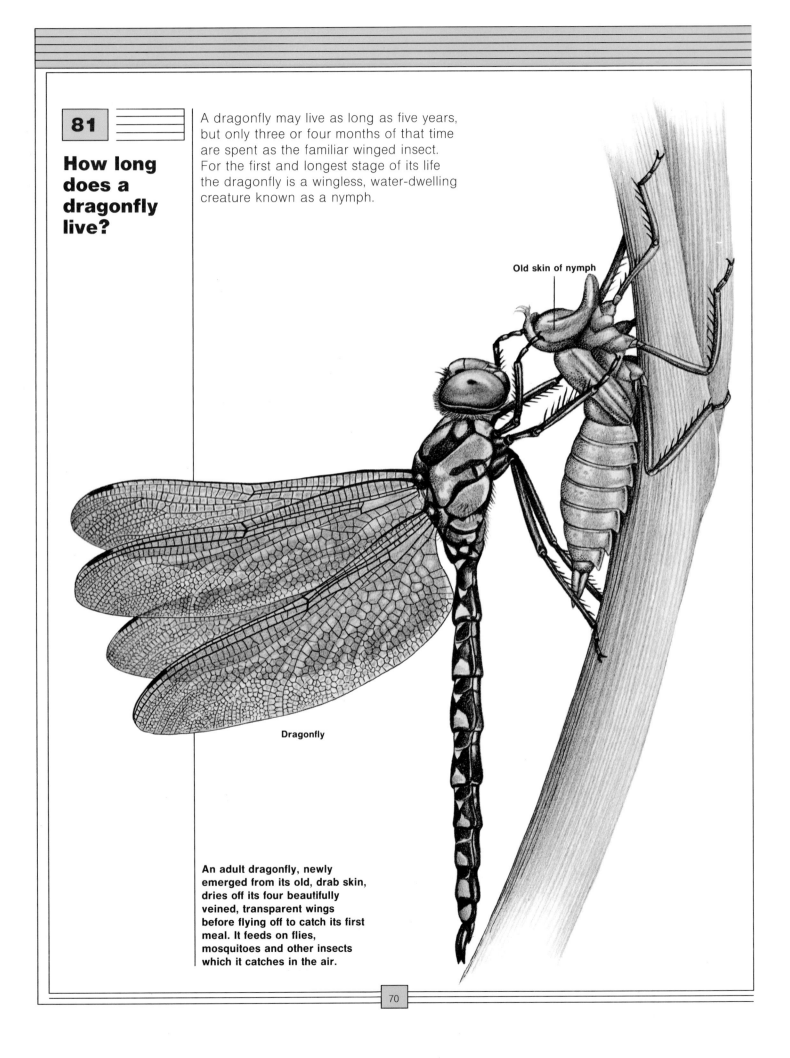

81

How long does a dragonfly live?

A dragonfly may live as long as five years, but only three or four months of that time are spent as the familiar winged insect. For the first and longest stage of its life the dragonfly is a wingless, water-dwelling creature known as a nymph.

Old skin of nymph

Dragonfly

An adult dragonfly, newly emerged from its old, drab skin, dries off its four beautifully veined, transparent wings before flying off to catch its first meal. It feeds on flies, mosquitoes and other insects which it catches in the air.

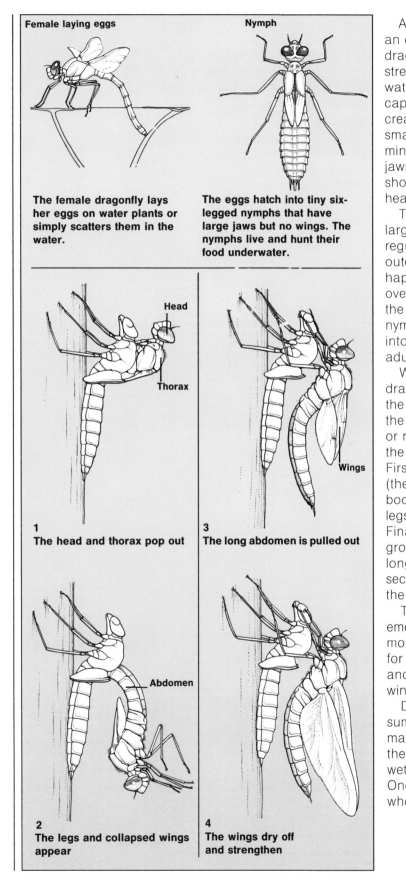

Female laying eggs

The female dragonfly lays her eggs on water plants or simply scatters them in the water.

Nymph

The eggs hatch into tiny six-legged nymphs that have large jaws but no wings. The nymphs live and hunt their food underwater.

Head

Thorax

1
The head and thorax pop out

Wings

3
The long abdomen is pulled out

Abdomen

2
The legs and collapsed wings appear

4
The wings dry off and strengthen

A nymph hatches from an egg laid by a female dragonfly in or close to a stream or lake. It lives in water and feeds by capturing other water creatures up to the size of small fish (such as young minnows) with its toothed jaws. These jaws can be shot out in front of the head.

To be able to grow larger the nymph must regularly shed its tough outer skin. This may happen ten to fifteen times over four or five years until the dull brown or gray nymph is ready to change into a brilliantly colored adult dragonfly.

When ready for its dramatic transformation, the nymph crawls up out of the water onto a plant stem or rock. Its skin splits along the middle of the back. First, the head and thorax (the middle section of the body) pop out; then the legs and collapsed wings. Finally, the dragonfly, with growing strength, pulls its long abdomen, the last section of its body, out of the old skin.

The new adult normally emerges in the early morning. It then has to wait for the rising sun to warm and dry its newly unfurled wings before it can fly off.

Dragonflies emerge in summer and must find a mate and lay eggs before they die in the cooler, wetter weather of autumn. Once the eggs are laid the whole cycle begins again.

82

Why are some animals awake at night?

Animals that wake up at night and sleep in the day do so for good reasons—for instance, to make sure they find enough food, to keep themselves cool, and to avoid other problems daytime brings. Animals that are active at night are described as nocturnal.

Owls are flying hunters, but most come out only at night when hawks and kestrels, which feed on the same sorts of food, are asleep. This way they avoid competing with their "rivals." Owls catch large insects, mice and other small

Long-eared owl

animals with the help of their huge eyes and sensitive ears. The superb ears of barn owls, for example, enable them to pinpoint the merest scratch of a moving mouse with great accuracy, even in complete darkness. At night, owls have the skies almost to themselves, except for the bats, which hunt for different prey.

Many desert-living rodents, such as jerboas, are nocturnal. The fierce daytime heat would harm and even kill them, so they stay in underground burrows where the air is cool and moist. Only at night, when the air above ground is cooler, do they come out. With their big eyes and large sensitive ears they find food in the dark while avoiding their own enemies.

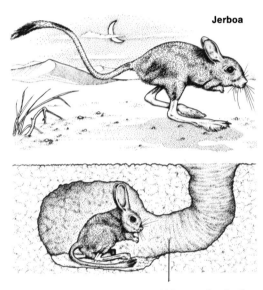

Jerboa

Cool, humid burrow for daytime

83

Do fish know when it's nighttime?

The way that some fish behave shows that they are affected by day and night and live in tune with the changes above the water.

Common sole, for example, swim about at night catching and eating worms and shellfish. At dawn they go back to their daytime resting spots where they lie half-buried on the sandy seabed. By camouflaging themselves in this way they also avoid the danger of being caught by fish hunting in the day.

Some light reaches to the depths where most coastal and shallow-water fish live, but in the deepest sea, five or six miles (8 to 9.5 km) down, there is no light at all. The fish that live there are probably unaffected by the cycles of day and night of the world above them.

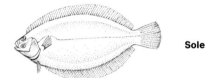

Sole

Common sole are fish that are affected by day and night. They hunt by night and lie asleep and hidden in the seabed by night.

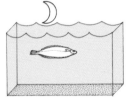

Night

Day

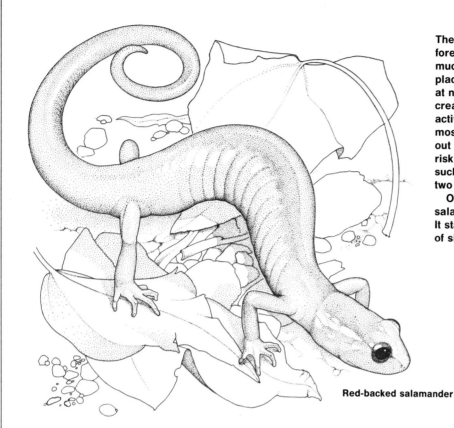

The red-backed salamander lives in cool moist forests of Canada and the United States. It spends much of the day asleep, hidden in cool moist places under fallen logs or stones, and comes out at night to hunt for insects and other small creatures. Although the salamander may be active for a while in the early morning, for the most part it avoids daylight. Warm sun would dry out its body and harm it. Also, in the daytime the risk of being caught by other hunting animals, such as foxes, is greater. So the salamander has two good reasons for being nocturnal.

On nights when there is a bright full moon the salamander's normal rhythm of activity changes. It stays quiet and hidden for much of the night, out of sight of keen-eyed nocturnal hunters.

Red-backed salamander

84

Why do fireflies flash?

The fireflies' flash of light is a mating signal. By flashing, male and female "talk" to each other through the darkness.

Fireflies are active at night so at mating time need a way of finding each other in the dark. On the underside of the firefly's body is a light organ. Chemical reactions in this organ make a cool, greenish light. The flashes of light are triggered by nerve impulses, and each kind of firefly has its own particular pattern and spacing of flashes, rather like Morse code.

Male fireflies make courtship flights, flashing their particular signal until they are "answered" by females of the same kind.

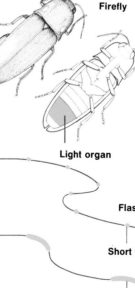

Firefly

Light organ

At dusk the male fireflies fly around just above ground flashing their signals. Females watch from the ground or a nearby bush. When a female recognizes the pattern of her own kind she answers with the same pattern of flashes. The male then knows exactly where to land to find her.

The diagrams below show the flash patterns of four kinds of firefly.

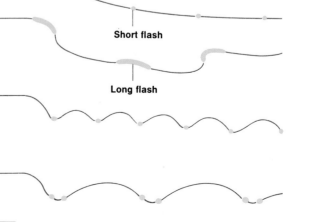

Flash patterns of 4 different kinds of firefly

Short flash

Long flash

85

Why do we sleep?

Everyone needs sleep but no one really knows why. Many people have tried, without success, to live without it and to find out why it is so essential.

Part of the reason might be that human beings are most active and most efficient in the daytime. Eyesight is important in almost everything we do, and in complete darkness we are relatively helpless compared with bats, owls and mice.

It seems to make sense that we are programmed to be less active at night, but why we should fall into a state of near-unconsciousness is not clear.

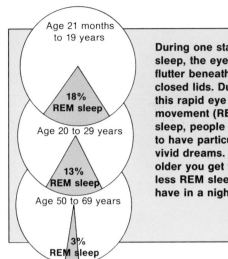

Age 21 months to 19 years

18% REM sleep

Age 20 to 29 years

13% REM sleep

Age 50 to 69 years

3% REM sleep

During one stage of sleep, the eyes flutter beneath closed lids. During this rapid eye movement (REM) sleep, people seem to have particularly vivid dreams. The older you get the less REM sleep you have in a night.

86

What makes me sleepy?

Your body is programmed to have regular periods of sleep, and sleep is something you can't go without for long. An internal or body clock in the brain (see page 78) controls this waking-sleeping rhythm in your life. Even when there are no outside clues such as darkness, light or clocks, this body clock is able to "turn on" sleeping and waking periods at the correct intervals in every 24 hours.

When your body clock says it's time for a sleep period, you feel sleepy. When it says it is time for a period of wakefulness, you wake up. Experiments in which volunteers are kept in closed rooms or dark caves with no clues about time outside have shown the power of this body rhythm. The people went to sleep at about the same time every day at intervals of about 24 hours. Over a long period that interval turned out to be nearer 25 hours, showing that the body's clock runs to a slightly different length of day than a mechanical clock.

The body's controls make sure that you do not lose sleep for too long. Even if you manage to force yourself to stay awake for 48 hours or so, the feeling of sleepiness soon becomes overpowering. When you do finally fall asleep you sleep for longer than usual as if to "catch up."

If people are kept away from light and other time clues, they sleep and wake at regular times. However, as the diagram shows, their cycle gradually drifts out of phase with the outside time.

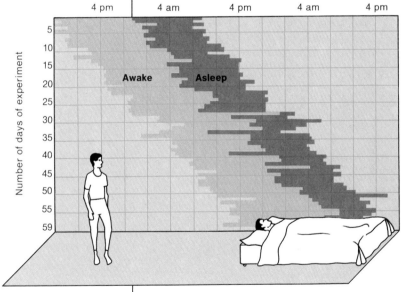

Number of days of experiment

Awake   Asleep

87

What is a dream?

A dream is a set of experiences—often strange, crazy ones—remembered from when we are asleep. Probably everyone has dreams every night, but some people are better at remembering and describing their dreams than others. People woken from rapid eye movement (REM) sleep can nearly always describe their dreams.

Dreams often seem so real that we feel they must have some meaning. Some scientists think that a dream is the brain's way of trying to make sense of everything that has happened the previous day and trying to find a pattern to the complex events of life. As yet, however, no one knows whether or not this idea is true.

What is going on in my head when I'm asleep?

Each stage of sleep is identified by the electrical activity of the brain. When the brain activity of a sleeping person is monitored by machine, the "brain waves" change with each stage. Rapid eye movement (REM) sleep has its own pattern of spiky waves.

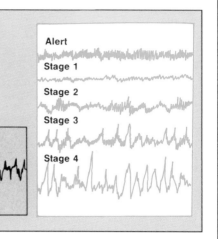

Alert
Stage 1
Stage 2
Stage 3
Stage 4

Waves traced by the brain's activity during REM sleep

When you are asleep your brain is certainly not switched off. You are in an unusual mental state someway between full wakefulness and the sort of unconsciousness that happens if you get knocked out by a blow on the head. When someone is unconscious, the brain is not working fully—it can only control the vital functions of the body that make the difference between life and death, such as breathing and heart beat. Things happening around an unconscious person will not rouse them.

When you are asleep, even though you may look unconscious, certain things will immediately wake you. Someone muttering nonsense in a low voice will not wake you. Someone saying your name urgently probably will. It seems that even while you are asleep your brain is still taking in information about the outside world from your senses but it is ignoring nearly all of it.

Every night, a sleeping person goes through four cyclic stages of different depths of sleep. Each complete cycle takes about 80 to 100 minutes and recurs four or five times a night. The rapid eye movement (REM) sleep, associated with vivid dreams, happens at the shallowest period of sleep.

The stages of sleep are measured and identified by the amount of electrical activity in the brain. A special machine can record the electrical waves from the scalp of a sleeping person.

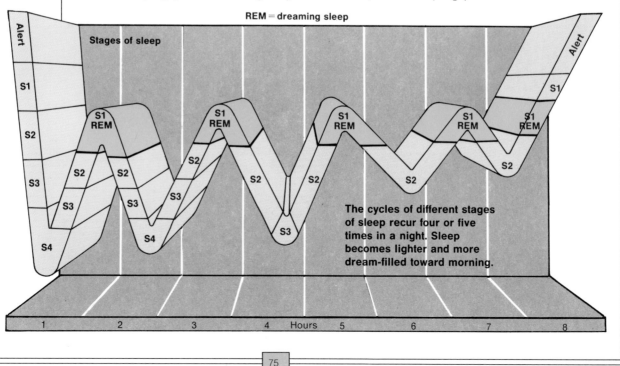

REM = dreaming sleep

Stages of sleep

Alert
S1
S2
S3
S4

The cycles of different stages of sleep recur four or five times in a night. Sleep becomes lighter and more dream-filled toward morning.

Hours 1 2 3 4 5 6 7 8

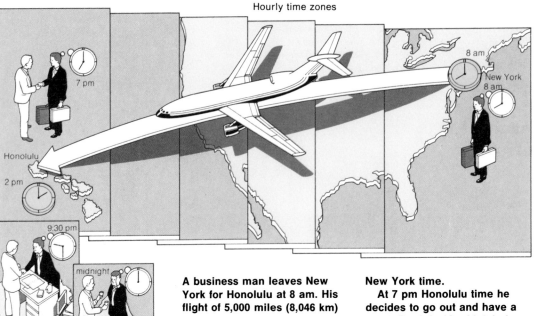

Hourly time zones

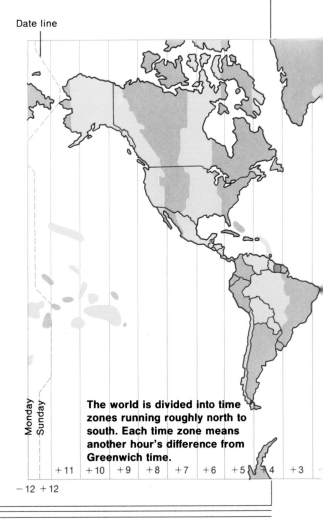

A business man leaves New York for Honolulu at 8 am. His flight of 5,000 miles (8,046 km) across five time zones takes about 11 hours and he arrives in Honolulu at 2 pm their time. His body clock, though, is at 7 pm New York time.

At 7 pm Honolulu time he decides to go out and have a meal. But it is 12 midnight by his body clock and he is really too tired to eat and enjoy himself.

Jet lag is the feeling of unusual tiredness and confusion felt by many air travelers after a long flight. You feel much worse after a journey made east or west around the world than after one north or south.

The problem is not just caused by a long, boring flight or by the strangeness of a new country. If it were, the effects would be the same whatever your flight direction. The feeling of jet lag seems to be caused by moving east or west across the Earth's time zones and by the body's reaction to the sudden change in the length of day or night. When you travel west, your day is lengthened. When you travel east, it is shortened. Either way, everything happens at a different time from the place you just came from.

The biological clock inside your body (see page 78) expects each day to be about 24 hours. Your body clock is in tune with night and day in your part of the world. Moving around the world means that your body clock has to be reset, and it is several days before this resetting is complete. Before that, all your body rhythms are "out of synch" with the world around you.

The world is divided into time zones running roughly north to south. Each time zone means another hour's difference from Greenwich time.

90

Why does jet lag make people feel bad?

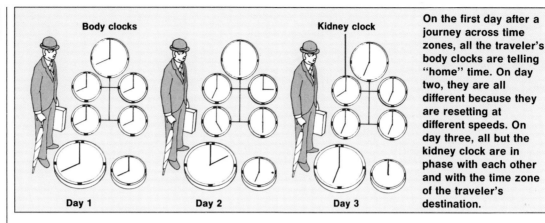

Body clocks

Kidney clock

Day 1   Day 2   Day 3

On the first day after a journey across time zones, all the traveler's body clocks are telling "home" time. On day two, they are all different because they are resetting at different speeds. On day three, all but the kidney clock are in phase with each other and with the time zone of the traveler's destination.

When you're jetlagged you feel hungry at the wrong time, sleepy at the wrong time, and so on. And the greater the difference between your body clock time and the real time in the place you have traveled to, the worse the feelings of jet lag.

The problem is made more complicated because there are several different body clocks that control different parts of the body. These include a sleep-wake clock, a clock controlling body temperature and the clock that keeps most kidney activity and urinating to the daylight hours. Each clock takes a different time to be reset after a long-haul trip.

For a few days, all the clocks are at different "times." Only when they have all caught up with each other do sleep patterns and other body functions return to normal.

91

Why is it breakfast time in New York when it's lunchtime in London?

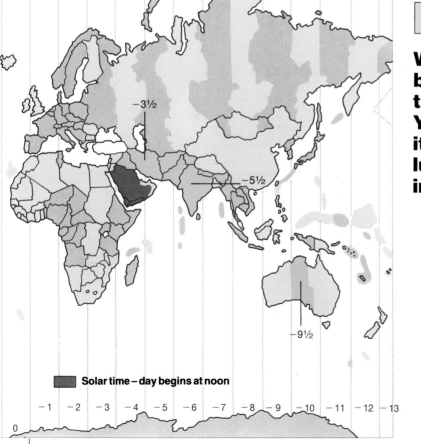

Solar time – day begins at noon

+1 0   −1   −2   −3   −4   −5   −6   −7   −8   −9   −10   −11   −12   −13

−3½

−5½

−9½

The Earth spins as it travels around the sun and makes one complete spin every 24 hours. Because of this, different places around the globe pass from dawn to noon to dusk at different times.

Each day starts in the mid-Pacific. Dawn then passes around the world from east to west. By the time breakfast is served in New York, London has moved on to lunch.

All the clocks of the world are set in advance or behind time at an imaginary line through Greenwich in England. The rest of the world is divided into time zone strips. Each zone means an hour's jump in time—five zones east of Greenwich the time is five hours later; five zones west it is five hours earlier.

92

Can I think better at certain times of day?

Many children and grown-ups find that they can think and concentrate better in the morning and feel less alert as the day goes on. Not everyone is quite the same, but a difference between morning and afternoon alertness, though small, does seem to exist.

Your ability to remember facts, work out tricky mathematical problems or even play a video game varies over 24 hours and this is a body rhythm.

Many of your body's workings and skills do not stay at the same level through the day and night. Brain power skills usually peak around mid-morning. They tend to drop during the afternoon and evening and reach their low in the middle of the night.

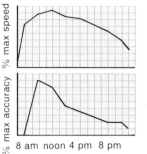

The graphs show that performance in multiplication tests is fastest and most accurate in the morning.

93

Why do I wake up at about the same time every day?

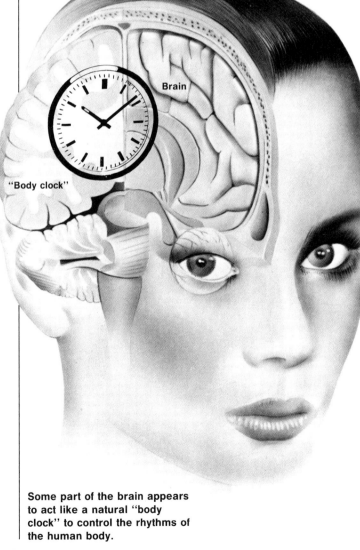

Some part of the brain appears to act like a natural "body clock" to control the rhythms of the human body.

Even if there were no such things as alarm clocks, you would probably find that you would wake at much the same time every day because your own body tells you to.

Experiments have tested this. Volunteers have been shut up in rooms with no daylight, only electric light, and no clock or other clues to tell them how fast time is passing. They were then watched to see how they divided their days and nights.

In experiments like these the people go to sleep and wake up at much the same time every day. This shows that the human body has its own "clock," probably somewhere in the brain. Our biological clock, as it is known, helps us keep the rhythmical parts of our lives, such as sleeping and waking, properly organized.

In fact, the biological clock seems to run to a day slightly longer than 24 hours. People in the experiments tend to gradually "drift" out of phase with outside time.

94

Why is my sister tired in the evening when I still feel good?

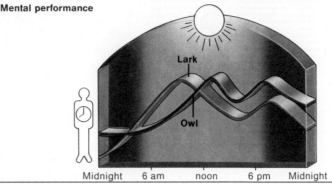

Mental performance

Lark

Owl

Midnight   6 am   noon   6 pm   Midnight

The graph shows the daily rhythm of peaks and lows of mental ability for a typical "owl" and a typical "lark."

If the difference is there every day, even though you have done much the same things, it may be that you and your sister have slightly different daily rhythms of alertness.

All sorts of brain and body activities vary from person to person. Some people are better than others at playing the violin, running a race or remembering lines in a play. Although practice and training can improve performance, people are born with certain characteristics.

Body rhythms, partly controlled by the clocks in the brain, vary just as abilities do. People taking part in the "locked room" experiments (see page 74) are found to live to slightly different day lengths when left to follow their own natural body clocks. One person might have a day of 24 hours and 15 minutes, another of as much as 25 hours. If the length of the body's day can vary, the pattern of alertness during it probably can too.

Although such differences should not be exaggerated, people are often said to divide into "larks" and "owls" because of their different alertness cycles. Larks love the morning. They spring out of bed full of energy and are soon at their peak. By contrast, owls find it hard to get up and are slower in the morning, but they are more lively and alert until later in the day than larks.

Most people are probably somewhere between these two extremes.

95

Is my body always the same temperature?

Yes, more or less. The human body is very good at keeping itself at a temperature of around 97.5 to 98.8 degrees Fahrenheit (36.3 to 37.1 degrees Centigrade).

Sophisticated control centers in the brain act as living thermostats and keep the temperature around this level.

There is, though, a daily rhythm of body temperature with a change of only about 1 degree F (0.5 degree C). The temperature is lowest in the morning just before waking, and highest around 9 pm.

Greater changes are unusual and can be dangerous. When you are ill, the temperature may rise a few degrees. Equally dangerous can be a drop in temperature if the body gets extremely cold. This condition is called hypothermia.

The graph shows the daily rhythm of body temperature as recorded in a group of normal people over a period of several days.

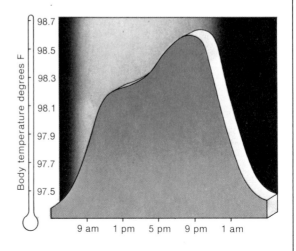

Body temperature degrees F

98.7
98.5
98.3
98.1
97.9
97.7
97.5

9 am   1 pm   5 pm   9 pm   1 am

Why does my tummy rumble?

The stomach and intestines (the tube leading from the stomach) are made partly of muscles that tighten and relax in a regular, rhythmic way to push food along. It is air in these tubes that makes rumbling noises.

Imagine trying to push a bead through a straw or tube. You would keep squeezing the part of the tube just behind the bead to force it along. The intestines work in the same way, but your muscles do the squeezing. The waves of muscle action they make are called peristalsis.

There are always some air and gas bubbles in the stomach and intestines and when these are squeezed by peristalsis they can cause loud rumbling and gurgling noises. This can happen whether or not there is any food in the system.

The waves of muscle action that push food through the digestive system start at the back of the throat when you first swallow a mouthful of food. The food is pushed down your gullet into your stomach.

The stomach's muscles churn the food up and mix it with substances which help break down the food.

Below the stomach more rhythmic muscle actions take the food through the small and large intestines. Here, more substances, such as enzymes and bile, are added to complete the breakdown of the food. The undigested remains pass out of the body some 12 to 24 hours after the food was first swallowed.

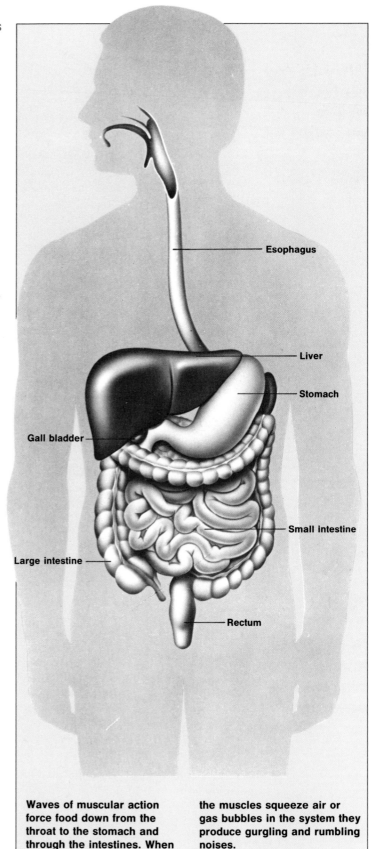

Waves of muscular action force food down from the throat to the stomach and through the intestines. When the muscles squeeze air or gas bubbles in the system they produce gurgling and rumbling noises.

Do animals eat three meals a day like we do?

No, they don't. Every kind of animal has its own eating habits that depend on how much energy that animal needs and what food it can find.

Rich foods, containing lots of protein, fats and sugars, can keep an animal going for a long time. The meat and fat in the bodies of other animals are rich foods like this. Large hunting animals, such as lions, big snakes and eagles, can catch good-sized prey animals and gorge themselves on the protein-stuffed flesh. One good meal may keep the hunter satisfied for several days.

In contrast, animals that eat plant food may have to feed almost constantly to get enough nourishment. Cows and sheep are examples of this type of animal.

How often an animal eats also depends on how much energy it uses. Warm-blooded animals, mammals and birds, need energy to keep their bodies warm and must have enough food to provide this energy. Small animals cool down faster than large ones, and can take in only small amounts of food at a time, so

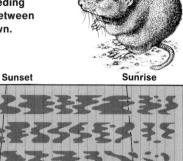

Short-tailed vole

Voles feed little and often. Their longest periods of feeding usually fall between dusk and dawn.

Sunset | Sunrise

1pm 5pm 9pm 1am 5am 9am

must have frequent meals to keep energy levels high.

Many small animals spend most of their waking hours searching for and eating food. Voles feed on seeds and berries every couple of hours. Tiny shrews are constantly hunting insects, worms and snails. If they are unable to find food for even a few hours they are likely to die of hunger.

Lions, particularly when hunting in groups, can bring down animals as big as zebra, wildebeest and buffalo. Such large prey keep the lions going for a couple of days.

Lion

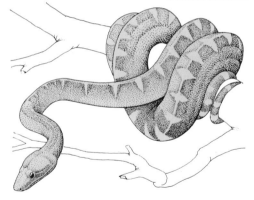

Emerald tree boa

Like many snakes, this tree boa, has flexible jaws which separate in the middle. This allows the snake to swallow prey animals which are bigger than its own head. After such a large meal, the snake may not need to eat again for several days.

How fast does my heart beat?

The number of times your heart beats each minute depends on how old you are and what you are doing or thinking. A baby's heart can race along at about 120 beats a minute while a child's beats 90 to 100 times. Once you are grown up, the rate has slowed to only 70 or 80 beats a minute.

The heart is a pump made of muscles that squeeze blood through the arteries and veins running throughout the body. Each squeeze is a heartbeat you feel as a thump in your chest or a pulse at your wrist. The heart speeds up when you are active or anxious but must never fail if you are to stay alive.

If you could count the heartbeats during an average person's lifespan the number would be about five billion.

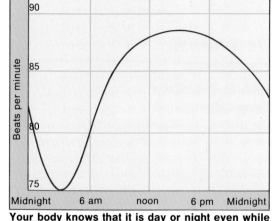

Your body knows that it is day or night even while you are asleep. The brain "tells" the heart to slow down at night and to speed up during the day. These changes match the blood flow around the body to your needs—lower at night, higher by day—as the graph shows.

Why does my heart beat faster when I run?

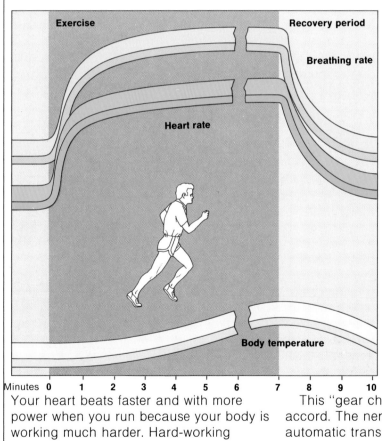

When you start to run not only does your heart beat faster but your breathing quickens too. The blood picks up its oxygen from the lungs. Faster, deeper breaths bring more oxygen-rich air into the lungs and more oxygen into the blood. With both lungs and heart working harder at the same time, there is a quick increase in the flow of oxygen from the lungs, via the blood, to the muscles that need it so urgently.

Muscles need oxygen to provide energy for the work they do. Every muscle action means that more fuel, in the form of oxygen, is needed. The muscles use oxygen to "burn" glucose and make the energy to do their work.

Your heart beats faster and with more power when you run because your body is working much harder. Hard-working muscles use more energy than resting ones and this energy must come from oxygen carried in the bloodstream. The faster the heart beats the more blood it circulates and the more oxygen gets to the muscles.

This "gear change" happens of its own accord. The nervous system acts like automatic transmission in a car, changing gear, when required, on its own. When you run or do something energetic the heart starts to beat faster and with more strength. You cannot stop this happening by thinking about it. At the end of the activity the heart rate returns to normal.

100

How often does my cat's heart beat?

An adult cat lying dozing in the sun has a heart rate of about 200 beats a minute. If it runs off after a bird its heart rate goes up to 300 or so.

In warm-blooded animals (mammals and birds), heartbeat rates are generally linked to body size. So big animals have slow heart rates, small animals much faster ones. Heartbeat rate is also related to the life the animal leads. Creatures that use lots of energy running or flying need faster beating hearts than slow-moving animals.

Shrews, for example, are small and constantly active; they have heart rates of as much as 800 beats a minute. Tiny-bodied bats have heartbeat rates of 660 to provide the huge amount of energy they need to fly. Birds have high heartbeat rates for the same reason. A starling, for example, has a heart rate of 400 beats a minute.

Of the bigger animals, a seal's heart beats 100 times a minute. The ostrich, the largest of all birds, has a heartbeat rate of only 65. The largest land mammal, the elephant, has a rate of 30, well below that of man.

The heartbeat rates of cold-blooded creatures, such as fish, reptiles and frogs, vary with the temperature around them. A crocodile's heart beats only 30 times a minute at 60 degrees Fahrenheit (15 degrees Centigrade)—a cool nighttime temperature in Africa—but rises to 70 beats at a temperature of 75 degrees F (24 degrees C).

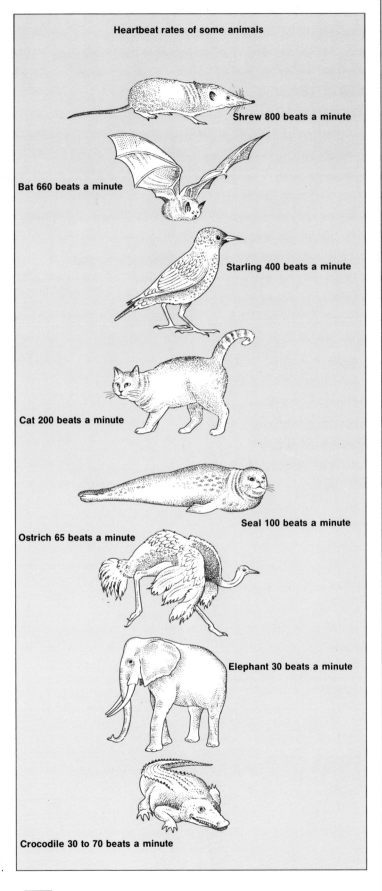

Heartbeat rates of some animals

Shrew 800 beats a minute

Bat 660 beats a minute

Starling 400 beats a minute

Cat 200 beats a minute

Seal 100 beats a minute

Ostrich 65 beats a minute

Elephant 30 beats a minute

Crocodile 30 to 70 beats a minute

101

How often do I take a breath?

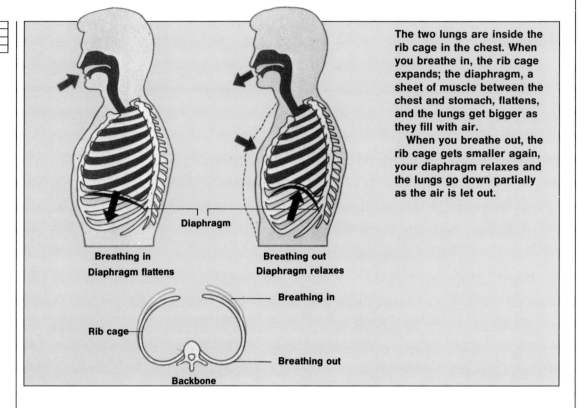

The two lungs are inside the rib cage in the chest. When you breathe in, the rib cage expands; the diaphragm, a sheet of muscle between the chest and stomach, flattens, and the lungs get bigger as they fill with air.

When you breathe out, the rib cage gets smaller again, your diaphragm relaxes and the lungs go down partially as the air is let out.

Diaphragm

Breathing in
Diaphragm flattens

Breathing out
Diaphragm relaxes

Breathing in

Rib cage

Breathing out

Backbone

You breathe about 12 to 15 times every minute. That is, you breathe in and breathe out again that many times. Each whole breath is made up of one air intake or inspiration, and one air exit or expiration. Breathing is a definite rhythm and all living people breathe continuously from the day they are born until the moment they die.

Breathing happens automatically. Even when you are asleep you are breathing. Then, the controller or "pacemaker" part of your brain is in sole—but safe—charge of breathing.

You can take charge over the automatic system and breathe as fast or slowly as you want, but only for a short time. After a minute or so of breath holding, or a period of fast panting, the body's automatic controls take over again and set up the correct rhythmic pace.

Your body's system of automatic controls also makes sure that your breathing rate matches the changing needs of your body. So, when you run around and need more oxygen you breathe more often each minute. When you are asleep and hardly moving your body is using very little oxygen and your breathing rate drops.

102

How long can I hold my breath?

Most people can hold their breath for about a minute—especially if they have taken some fast, deep breaths first to build up oxygen supplies in the body. The world record for breath holding is an amazing six minutes.

However hard you try to hold your breath, safety devices in your body soon force you to start breathing again. Sense cells in the blood vessels keep a check on the levels of gas in the blood. If breathing stops, the cells note the falling oxygen levels and rising carbon dioxide. They signal to the brain to quicken breathing.

The best breath holders of all are diving mammals such as whales. Their heart rates slow down while they are underwater and blood supply is shut off from all but the most essential organs so they use little oxygen. In this way, whales can hold their breath for as much as 30 minutes or more while diving deep under the sea to find food. Usually, though, they make much briefer dives.

What are lungs made of?

The lungs are made of soft spongy body tissue. Like sponges they contain millions of tiny spaces which fill with air in the same way as a sponge fills with water in the bath tub.

When you breathe in, the small spaces get bigger to make room for the incoming air. When you breathe out, the spaces collapse a little. The air gets in and out of the lungs through the windpipe or trachea which you can feel as a knobbly tube at the center of your throat.

The reason why you have to breathe is to get oxygen into the bloodstream so that it can be taken to every part of the body (see page 82). So, the lungs must have a good supply of blood vessels as well as air spaces.

Blood which has been all around the body and has given up its oxygen is pumped by the heart to the lungs. Here it picks up oxygen from the air that has been breathed in. At the same time it gives up a waste gas, carbon dioxide, which is breathed out. Filled with oxygen and cleansed of its waste, the blood passes back to the heart to be pumped around the body again.

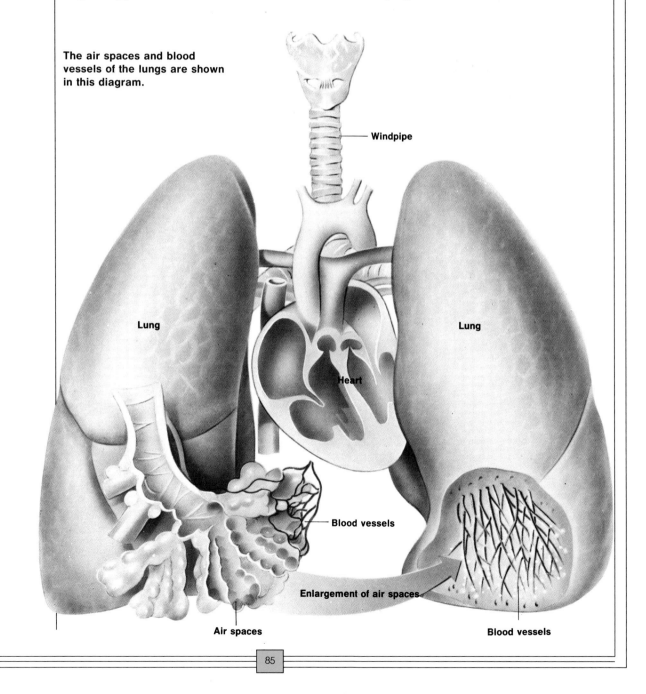

The air spaces and blood vessels of the lungs are shown in this diagram.

Windpipe

Lung

Lung

Heart

Blood vessels

Enlargement of air spaces

Air spaces

Blood vessels

Why do animals become extinct?

An extinction means the death of a whole kind or species of animal. Animals that are extinct will never return. Extinctions happen when more of those animals die than are born until eventually the species disappears. There are two main causes of extinctions: change and competition.

When something happens to change the place where an animal lives, its chances of surviving and being the parent of young may be reduced. For example, there may be a change in climate. If the weather in an area gets steadily wetter or drier, hotter or colder, some animals will not be able to cope with the new conditions. If they are unable to migrate somewhere else their numbers will fall. Eventually the animals will disappear as dying adults are unable to rebuild their numbers with new young.

When two different sorts of animal are competing for the same food, shelter or other necessity of life, and one is much more successful than the other, the "underdog" will eventually die out.

Unfortunately, human beings are also the cause of many extinctions, either by killing creatures in large numbers or by drastically changing the places where they live—destroying huge areas of forest, for example.

Other than the damage caused by human beings, the reasons for extinctions were just the same millions of years ago, when dinosaurs and other prehistoric animals lived and died, as they are now. Extinctions have always been a natural part of life on Earth. In fact, more kinds of animals have become extinct than at present exist.

Today's mammals may be descended from prehistoric reptiles such as Kannemeyeria which lived about 240 million years ago.

Kannemeyeria

A primitive reptile which lived 280 million years ago, Dimetrodon was a powerful hunter with ferocious teeth. By 250 million years ago these animals were extinct.

Dimetrodon

105

Why did the dodo die?

The dodo once lived on the island of Mauritius but became extinct in 1681 because of the interference of man.

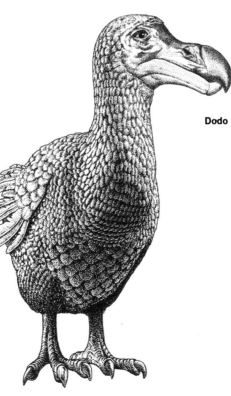

Dodo

The extinction of the dodo is a frightening example of the impact of human beings on the survival of animal life on our planet.

The dodo lived on the island of Mauritius in the Indian Ocean. A clumsy-looking bird about the size of a large turkey, it had a large head and beak and short, strong legs. It had tiny wings and could not fly.

When European sailors first landed on the island in the sixteenth century they thought the birds stupid because they had no fear of man. The slow-moving dodos were easy prey and the men killed them relentlessly for food.

The new human arrivals also introduced pigs and rats to the island. These destroyed the eggs and nestlings of the dodos so they could no longer breed successfully. This, combined with the large numbers killed, led to dodos being extinct by 1681, just 82 years after they were first discovered by Europeans.

Now the dodo lives on only in the phrase "dead as a dodo," used to describe something that is truly dead and gone.

What is a second?

A second does not correspond exactly to any natural feature of the Earth or its movement. But the heart of an adult human beats about once every second.

For scientists all over the world the second is extremely important as the standard unit of time. In experiments where the greatest accuracy is needed, the second is related to the number of vibrations that occur in some atoms. (An atom is the smallest particle of any substance.) In the right conditions these fast vibrations are also very regular, so it is possible to say how many occur in a second and use them to control a clock.

The atomic clock, the most advanced timepiece, makes use of the vibrations of atoms as its pacemaker. This clock is so accurate that in 30,000 years it would lose less than a second.

What are minutes and hours?

A minute is 60 seconds. An hour is 60 minutes. Neither relate to any natural rhythms but are convenient ways of dividing up the day. They are measured accurately in seconds.

What is a day?

One day and night is the time it takes for the Earth to spin once around its axis (see page 14). Humans divide the day into 24 hours and the sun sets and rises at 24-hour intervals.

At present, the Earth actually takes about 24 hours and 4 minutes to make a complete spin. The Earth keeps good time and this spin rate is extremely steady.

But very, very gradually the Earth's spin is slowing down. Evidence drawn from fossils—the remains of prehistoric animals or plants that have hardened to rock—of 400 million years ago suggests that then the day was only 22 hours long. If this is so the Earth has been slowing at the rate of two-thousandths of a second each century.

What is a week?

A week is now seven days but has not always been so. In the past, weeks have been as short as four days and as long as ten. Weeks are not based on any natural rhythm of the Earth but are "man-made."

Lit (daytime side of Earth)

Dark (nighttime side of Earth)

Moon's orbit

Illustrated above are the positions of the Earth, sun and moon during a year. The Earth orbits the sun once in a year, and the moon orbits the Earth once every 27.32 days. The images of the Earth show that at any instant, half the globe is lit by the sun (daytime) and the other half is in darkness (nighttime).

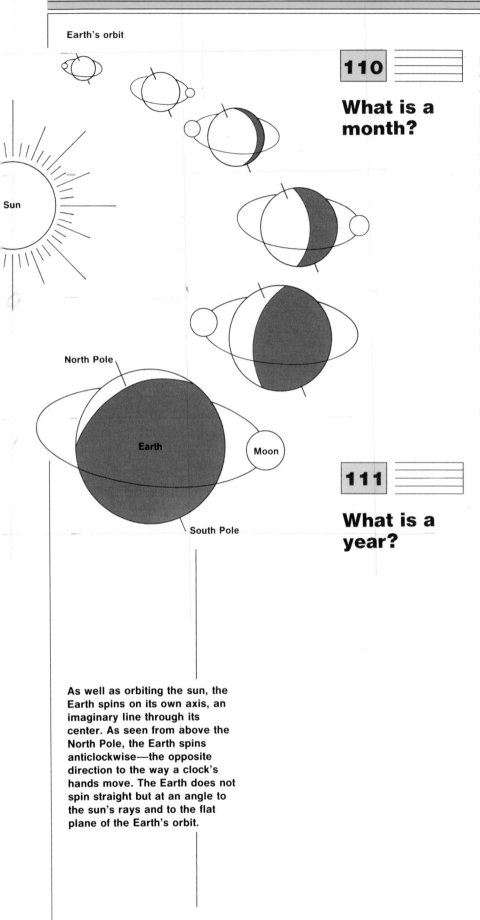

Earth's orbit

Sun

North Pole

Earth

Moon

South Pole

As well as orbiting the sun, the Earth spins on its own axis, an imaginary line through its center. As seen from above the North Pole, the Earth spins anticlockwise—the opposite direction to the way a clock's hands move. The Earth does not spin straight but at an angle to the sun's rays and to the flat plane of the Earth's orbit.

110

What is a month?

Months do relate to an important cycle in the heavens—the time it takes the moon to make a complete orbit around the Earth. At the moment, the length of time between one new moon and the next is about 29.53 days. The actual time it takes the moon to make its orbit is slightly less—27.32 days. The difference between the two is the result of the Earth's spin.

The modern calendar has months of a mixture of lengths—28, 29, 30 and 31 days. This is because there is not an exact number of moon cycles in a year. If the lengths of the months were not slightly adjusted, the months and the yearly seasons would slowly drift out of step with each other. But the average length of the twelve months in a year is just under 30.5 days, very close to the interval between two new moons.

The evidence of fossils from 400 million years ago suggests that the moon once orbited the Earth slightly more slowly than it does now. Then its orbit took nearly 31 days instead of the present 27.

111

What is a year?

A year is the amount of time our planet takes to complete one orbit or journey around the sun, and is an important unit of time on Earth.

At present, that journey takes 365.2 days. By having a leap year in which one day is added to the month of February every four years, making it 29 instead of 28 days, we get to an average year length of 365.25 days. This is close to the real orbit year. To cope with the slight difference between the two, tiny adjustments in time have to be agreed worldwide every so often.

The year reveals itself in the natural world around us as the march of the seasons and the repeating cycle of lengthening and shortening daylight hours. Once a year the sun reaches its highest point in the sky at noon and day length is at its longest. And once a year, too, the sun reaches its lowest noon position and day length is its shortest. One whole cycle of the seasons lasts one year.

As the Earth orbits the sun, we see the sun against each of twelve evenly spaced star groups once in each year. Each group has a name and these are the signs of the zodiac. The star group the sun appears to be in when you are born is your star sign.

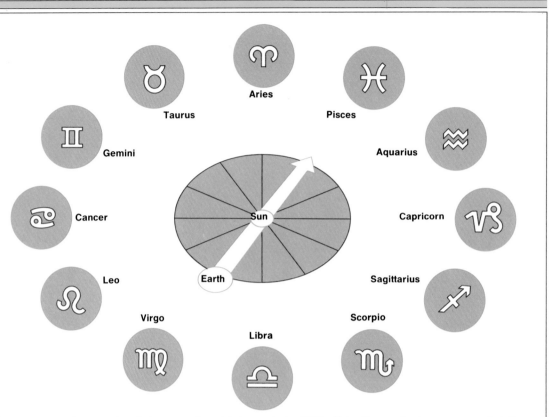

What is astrology?

Astrology is the study of the way in which the cycles of movement of the stars and planets in the sky are supposed to influence the lives and personalities of all of us on Earth.

The first astronomers and astrologers thought that the Earth was the center of the universe and that everything in the sky revolved around it. They believed that the sun circled the Earth and in doing so passed in front of twelve different groups or constellations of stars. Each of these star groups has a name and these are the signs of the zodiac into which astrologers divide the year—Aries, Leo, Gemini and so on. The group of stars the sun appears to be passing through when you are born is your star sign. Astrologers believe that this sign influences your future and your personality.

We now know of course that it is the Earth that orbits the sun not the other way around (see page 12). Because the position of the Earth is changing, the sun appears to be in different parts of the sky from our viewpoint.

An astrological "picture" of an individual's life and future is called a horoscope. For a complete horoscope to be drawn up, the exact time and place of the person's birth is needed as well as the date. With this, the astrologer can plot the position of all the planets in the sky at the moment of that person's birth. Each is supposed to have its own meaning and influence on future life. The position of the planets relative to each other is also held to be an important influence (see the diagram opposite).

Although many people enjoy reading their star sign predictions in newspapers or magazines, few really believe them. Imagine two babies of different parents who happen to be born at the same minute in the same maternity unit. Astrological predictions for both would be identical and their lives and personalities should be amazingly similar.

All that we now know about human life tells us that this cannot be true. Babies inherit their characteristics of personality and appearance from their parents. Their lives and behavior are also shaped by how and where they are raised. The two babies born at the same minute but of different parents will almost certainly have completely different lives.

The belief many people have in astrology can be traced back to the beginnings of astrology and scientific astronomy, which are linked together. Thousands of years ago the learned men who observed the movement of planets and stars in the sky were the only people able to predict the details of changing seasons and extraordinary events like eclipses (see page 25). Because they could predict these things, it was tempting to believe that they could also predict a person's future from star and planet movements.

Although common sense—and science—tells us astrology is nonsense, many people remain fascinated by it. But statistical surveys suggest there is nothing in it.

One sample of 300 people showed no clear relation between the astrological predictions made for them and actual events in their lives.

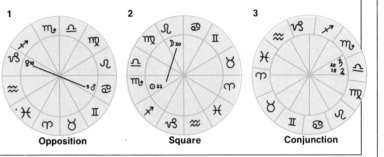

The position of the planets relative to each other is supposed to influence an individual horoscope. Planets in opposite sectors are said to create tension. Two at right angles can bring problems or give energy. Two in the same sector modify each other.

1 Opposition   2 Square   3 Conjunction

What are biorhythms?

The biorhythm idea tries to explain why we feel different from day to day; why we have ups and downs. It says that our lives are ruled by three different cycles of fitness. Each cycle is a different length and all three are supposed to begin on the day of our birth and last until we die.

The three cycles are physical well-being, with a 23-day cycle, emotional health, with a 28-day cycle, and intellectual ability, with a 33-day cycle. Each cycle is supposed to move through a good and bad or positive and negative phase. The point at which it moves from one to the other is thought to be difficult or "critical" for that person. About once every six months all three rhythms may be critical together, and such days, if the biorhythms theory is to be believed, are particularly bad.

The idea of biorhythms began in the late nineteenth century when an Austrian doctor, Hermann Swoboda, thought he could see a rhythmic pattern in the way his patients behaved. From his observations he decided that there were two cycles—emotional and physical. A German scientist later added a third, the intellectual biorhythm, to the list.

Most scientists, however, believe that there is no truth at all in the biorhythm theory and no evidence to support its claims.

Biorhythms are completely different from biological rhythms such as those of body temperature, heart beat and others (see pages 78 to 83). Each of these natural rhythms has been proved in careful experiments, and each fits in with the rest of our knowledge about how the human body works.

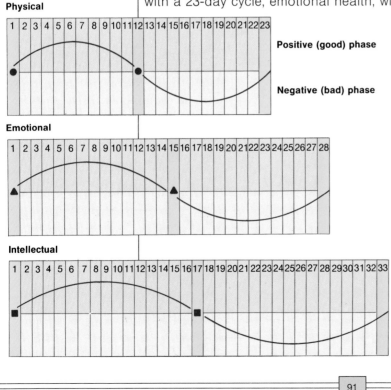

Physical

Positive (good) phase

Negative (bad) phase

Emotional

Intellectual

Index

Page numbers in bold type
indicate illustrations

lemming 67, **67**
Lepidoptera 44
lichens 34
lion 81, **81**
liverworts 34
locust 66, **66**
lungs, structure of 85, **85**

M

maize 34, **34**, 43
mammals 63, 81, 83
mammoth, woolly 17, **17**
Mars **12**, 13, 14
mayfly **68**, 69
Mediterranean Sea 21
Mercury **12**, 13, 14
meristem cells 35, 43
meteors 27
mice 63, 69
microbes 30
migration 48, 49
minute 88
mite, itch **69**
monkey 63, **68**
month 89
moon, conditions on 19
    eclipse of 25, **25**
    effect on tide of 20
    gravity of 19
    men on 19
    orbit of 18, 89
    phases of 18, **18**
mosquito 58, **58**
    hum of 58
mosses 33, 34
moths 44, 45
mushrooms 33
mussels 23

N

nectar 32, 36, 37
Neptune **13**, 14
nitrogen 10
nocturnal animals 72
North Pole 10, 14, 15, 16, 28, 88
northern lights 10

O

ostrich 83, **83**
ovule 34
owls 72
    barn 72
    long-eared **72**
oxygen 10, 82, 84, 85

P

Pacific 21
peristalsis 80
pheromone 56
photosynthesis 30, 31, 34, 40
pig **69**
pine trees 33, 41
    bristlecone **33**, 42
    Monterey **41**
pinworm 69
planets 8, 9, 13
    beginnings of 8–9
    distances of 12–13
"plant eggs" 32, 34
Plow/Plough 11
Pluto 13, 27
polar bear **15**
Pole, geographic North 15
    geographic South 15
    magnetic North 15
    magnetic South 15
    North 10, 14, 15, 16, 28, 88
    South 10, 14, 15, 16, 28, 88
Pole Star (Polaris) 14
pollen 32, 33, 34, 36, 37
pollination 36, 38
pollinators 36
pupa 44

Q

queen butterfly 56, **56**

R

rabbits 63, 66, **66**, **69**
raccoons 48
rats 69
razor shells 23
reptiles 9, 83

S

salamander, red-backed 73, **73**
Saturn **13**, 14
sea anemone 23, 54
sea lion 60, 61
seals 15, 60, **60**, 83, 83
    elephant 61, **61**
seasons 89
    in hot countries 29
    reasons for 28–29
seaweed **20**, 33, 34
second 88
seeds 34
    fertilization of 34
    germination of 34

Acknowledgments

Artwork by

Richard Orr   Michael Woods
and

David Ashby   Norman Barber   John Bavosi   Eugene Fleury
Will Giles   George Glaze   Tony Graham   Lynn Hector
Hayward and Martin   Aziz Khan   Steve Kirk   Alan Male
Tom McArthur   David More   David Parker   Jim Robbins
Paul Saunders   Les Smith   Dick Twinney   Phil Weare

Photographs by

8 The Hale Observatories/Aldus Archive
11 US Naval Observatory/Science Photo Library
14 Hughes Aircraft Corp/TRH
18/19 Lick Observatory Photographs
19 Space Frontiers/Daily Telegraph Colour Library
21 Anthony Price/Ace Photo Agency
24 John Fairweather
26 Lick Observatory Photograph
36 John Shaw/Bruce Coleman
38 Don Pavey Collection
48 David C. Fritts/AA/Oxford Scientific Films
53 The Royal Photographic Society

You can also enjoy finding out fascinating facts about the animal kingdom in *Do Animals Dream*?

Haven't you ever wondered if animals dream? Do they play? Do they have families like ours? How do parrots talk? How do bees make honey? Why does a snake have a forked tongue? Why do rattlesnakes rattle? Do hummingbirds hum?

These are just a few of the many questions asked and answered in this stunning book with illustrations, drawings and diagrams by two of the world's foremost natural history artists. Each answer provides a depth of insight into the perennially popular animal kingdom.

Do Animals Dream? by Joyce Pope is published by Viking Kestrel in the USA and Canada, and by Michael Joseph in Great Britain, and Australia and New Zealand.